THE TEAM
STRIKES AGAIN

David Bedford was born in Devon, in the south-west of England in 1969.

David wasn't always a writer. First he was a football player. He played for two teams: Appleton FC and Sankey Rangers. Although these weren't the worst teams in the league, they never won anything!

After school, David went to university and became a scientist. His first job was in America, where he worked on discovering new antibiotics.

David has always loved to read and decided to start writing stories himself. After a while, he left his job as a scientist and began writing full time. His novels and picture books have been translated into many languages around the world.

David lives with his wife and two children in Norfolk, England.

THE TEAM
STRIKES AGAIN

David Bedford

Illustrated by Keith Brumpton

LITTLE HARE
www.littleharebooks.com

For David Francis
—DB

Little Hare Books
8/21 Mary Street, Surry Hills
NSW 2010 AUSTRALIA

www.littleharebooks.com

Superteam first published 2004
Banned! first published 2005
Masters of Soccer first published 2006

This edition published 2009

National Library of Australia
Cataloguing-in-Publication entry

Bedford, David, 1969-

The team strikes again / David Bedford ; illustrator: Keith Brumpton.

978 1 921272 84 4 (pbk.)

For primary school age.

Soccer—Juvenile fiction.

Brumpton, Keith.

823.92

Cover design by Bernadette Gethings
Set in 13.5/21 Giovanni by Asset Typesetting Pty Ltd
Additional typesetting by Clinton Ellicott
Printed in China by WKT Company Ltd.

5 4 3 2 1

Contents

Prof
Gertie

Darren

Harvey

Rita

Matt

Steffi

Mark 1

SUPERTEAM

Chapter 1

Harvey's fingers trembled as he handed over the money. He'd never seen so much in his life — and it was all his.

He tried to look relaxed while the shop assistant counted the handful of notes, but he began to sweat when she tipped up his piggy bank and started sorting his entire life savings into neat piles of coins. Was it enough? He'd checked it at least five times, but —

The shop assistant gave Harvey a small, grey padded case with a picture of an armadillo on the front.

Harvey felt his face growing hot. It was Monday, the day before the new school year started, and the shop was packed with people who'd do anything to own what Harvey was holding. He was sure they were all staring at him greedily.

"Th-thanks!" Harvey stammered, tucking the case safely under his arm and walking quickly from the shop. As soon as he was outside, he put his head down and sprinted towards home. He'd done it! He, Harvey Boots, had just bought a pair of Armadillo Aces, the best football boots *anyone* could buy.

Skidding into Baker Street, he saw his neighbour, Professor Gertie, leaning from the top window of her inventing tower.

"Bring them up!" she called. "Right away!"

Harvey pushed open the door to the tower and clambered up the twisting stairs to where Mark 1, the Football Machine, was waiting. He was Professor Gertie's greatest invention: a robot designed purely for playing football.

Mark 1 grabbed for the Armadillo case, but Harvey held it out of his reach.

"Awww," the robot complained in his strange, mechanical voice.

"Over here!" Professor Gertie was at her workbench. "I know how hard you saved for

5

those boots," she said. "And it would be a terrible shame to get them scuffed and muddy after your first game. So, especially for you, I've invented PAP. It stands for Polish And Protect."

She held up a sprayer Harvey had seen her use to water plants. Now it had skull-and-crossbones danger signs stuck on it.

Harvey's hands tightened on his Armadillos. Professor Gertie's inventions sometimes backfired. "Er, have you tested it?" he asked politely.

Professor Gertie tutted. "What do you think?" She raised a foot and showed him one of her ancient white sandals. They were usually grubby, but now they shone so brightly that Harvey's eyes hurt.

Harvey wanted to feel encouraged, but he had an urge to escape. How could he, though? Professor Gertie did everything she could for The Team. She'd invented Mark 1 for them and, as their trainer, he'd helped them win the league last season, and a trip to Soccer Camp.

"Don't worry," Professor Gertie said soothingly. "PAP is designed to help, not harm."

With a *whirrr!*, Mark 1 tugged the case from Harvey, unzipped it, and tipped the jet black Armadillo Aces onto the table. Professor Gertie lined them up in a patch of sunlight.

"They're magnificent!" she declared. "Now stand back …"

Mark 1 made an urgent blaring noise like a warning siren and dived behind the sofa.

Harvey didn't move. He couldn't take his eyes from the small Armadillo badges on the side of each boot. They looked so *perfect* …

Professor Gertie sprayed twice.

Harvey saw a rainbow through the mist of oily droplets. As each drop landed on the Aces, it left a wet, glistening spot. Harvey bent closer. The spots began to pop, sizzle and crack.

He jerked backwards as puffs of smoke erupted like tiny mushroom clouds. There was a smell like cheese and toilet cleaner and rotten fish. Harvey held his nose and looked pleadingly at Professor Gertie. Her eyes goggled despairingly back at him.

"But — you said you'd tested it!" shouted Harvey, coughing as the boots steamed, writhed and shrivelled into two shapeless black blobs.

"I did!" cried Professor Gertie. "As soon as I made it. Yesterday!"

She unscrewed the top of the plant sprayer, sniffed, then slumped onto her stool.

"What is it?" said Harvey. "What happened?"

"It's gone off," she said feebly. "Oh, Harvey, what have I *done*?"

Chapter 2

"Where are they?" said Darren as Harvey joined him and Rita on the pitch that evening. "You said you were getting Armadillos."

"Really?" said Rita, surprised. "But how can Harvey afford those?"

Harvey looked longingly at Darren's and Rita's boots. They both had new Power Strikes — not too expensive, but good enough. Harvey wished he'd bought the same — and not let Professor Gertie anywhere near them.

He sighed, and told Darren and Rita what had happened. Rita gave a short, shocked gasp. Darren hid his face behind his goalkeeper's gloves.

"Wait," Rita said, frowning. "I still don't understand …"

"They're *gone*!" Darren wailed. "Professor Gertie blew up Harvey's Armadillos!"

"Not that bit," said Rita, putting her hands on her hips. "How did you get a pair of Armadillo Aces in the first place?" she asked Harvey sternly.

Darren lowered his gloves. "He didn't steal them, if that's what you mean," he said. "Harvey *bought* them."

"Armadillos cost a fortune!" said Rita.

"I used my savings," said Harvey quickly.

"But how did you save enough —" Rita began.

"He got money for his birthday," interrupted Darren. "And he spent what his folks gave him to buy new school stuff."

"I'll just wear my old uniform again," Harvey explained. "I'm sure it will still fit."

"It had better," said Rita doubtfully. "And what about your old boots? Do they still fit?"

She pointed at the well-worn Power Juniors Harvey had on.

"They're a bit tight," admitted Harvey, crouching down to loosen the laces as the rest of The Team arrived. It was their first meeting to plan for the new season, and Harvey saw that everyone on The Team had new boots.

Most wore Power Strikes, but not Steffi. Her boots were glittery lilac, Harvey noticed, and they had "Primadonna" scrawled along the side. She had a second, bright pink pair dangling from one shoulder.

"I prefer not to wear the same colour every game," Harvey heard her explain to Matt.

Matt lifted a foot, and Harvey felt a shiver run through him when he saw the tiny Armadillo badge. "Aces are as good as *three* pairs all in one," Matt announced. Then he looked down at Harvey's boots. "You should get professional ones like these, Harv. You'd score more goals, easy. I don't know why you're still wearing Juniors."

"They're *so* yesterday," commented Steffi, wrinkling her nose as if Harvey's old boots smelled bad.

"They look like something out of a *museum*," agreed Matt.

"Harvey feels comfortable in them, that's all," said Darren defensively. "They're your lucky boots, aren't they, Harvey?"

Harvey didn't want to explain, so he nodded.

"Is this supposed to be our lucky kit, too?" said Steffi, pouting as she tried to smooth the creases from her shirt. "We look like we've just crawled out of a washing machine, and I feel crumply."

The Team were wearing shirts, shorts and socks made from Professor Gertie's Supercloth, which was supposed to never need washing. The problem was, Professor Gertie hadn't tested it with water, and when their kit got wet for the first time at Soccer Camp, The Team had been lost under a mountain of soap bubbles.

"Everyone makes mistakes," Harvey said gloomily. "Anyway, she rinsed out the soap, so we should be okay."

"I suppose we're stuck with it, then," sulked Steffi.

The Team passed a ball around to warm up. Every time Harvey kicked it, though, his squashed-up toes felt like they were being hit with a hammer. He tried a gentle flick to Rita — and howled in pain.

Howls of laughter came back like echoes from the side of the pitch where, Harvey saw with dismay, a crowd had gathered to watch. He recognised several players from other teams, including the captain of the Diamonds, Paul Pepper, who was in his class at school.

"Keep trying!" Paul Pepper jeered. "Practice makes perfect!"

"What are *they* doing here?" said Harvey.

"Checking us out," said Rita. "We're the team to beat this year. After all, last season we came from the bottom to the top of the league."

Aware that he was being watched, Harvey booted the ball high towards Matt — and crumpled to the ground, rolling in agony.

"I heard something snap!" Harvey yelped, gripping his left boot as he heard the spectators cheering. Then, closer to him, he heard someone chuckling.

"It's not funny!" Harvey told Rita through clenched teeth.

"Sorry!" Rita spluttered. "It's just …" She pointed at Harvey's foot and began chortling so hard she couldn't speak.

Harvey sat up — and saw that his big toe was waving in the air. It had poked clean through his boot and sock. "That's what made the snapping sound, then," he said, sighing.

Matt crouched beside him. "If you can wiggle it, it's not broken," he said knowledgeably.

Harvey wiggled his toe. "It's okay," he said.

"Phew!" said Rita. "The last thing we need at the start of the season is an injured captain."

"What we *really* need is a captain with a decent pair of boots," said Steffi glumly.

Harvey glanced from his useless Juniors to

The Team's worried faces. Then he blushed as the audience on the sidelines began singing, "Boot up, boot up, Har-vey Boots!", conducted by Paul Pepper.

Harvey stayed sitting on the grass. He didn't feel like getting up — things could only get worse. Then he saw that one of the group was walking towards him.

"That's Jackie Spoyle," whispered Rita. "Her dad owns Spoyle Sports shop. She goes to your school, doesn't she?"

Harvey nodded. He'd bought his Armadillos from Spoyle's, and Jackie had been there, choosing what she was now wearing: a black bodysuit with footballs dotted all over it.

"She lives in the big house on my street," Rita told him. "And she gets *everything* she wants. Last year it was her own gym to train in. The year before she had a horse and jumps. She always gets the best gear, too."

"Looks like she's decided to be a football star now," said Darren.

Harvey began to laugh, then stopped. He'd just seen Jackie Spoyle's silver boots. They had armadillos on the side, but they weren't Aces.

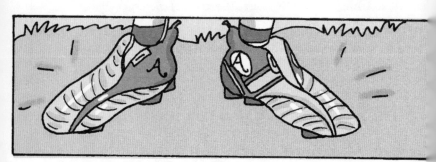

"These are Imps," Jackie told him. "They've only just come out and aren't even in the shops yet. But believe me, they're the *best*." She surveyed The Team, coughed lightly to clear her throat, and said, "I'm organising a new squad of players. An *elite* squad."

It took Harvey a moment to realise what she meant, but before he could respond, Rita beat him to it. "You're not pinching anyone from The Team!" she said hotly.

"Get outta here!" snorted Matt, swatting the air as if he was shooing away a fly.

Jackie looked Matt up and down, making a face as if she'd tasted something nasty. "I will be hand-picking the most promising talent," she said. "Some of you will be hearing from me again. Others, alas, will not."

Matt cackled as she walked away, but Harvey noticed that Steffi was watching Jackie with interest. "It makes sense, when you think about it," Steffi muttered. "She's *designing* a team."

"Designer rubbish won't beat us," said Darren gruffly.

Harvey wasn't so sure. It all depended on who Jackie Spoyle could get to play for her — and what she had to attract them with.

Suddenly, Jackie spun around. "You *do* know you're all wrinkly, don't you?" she asked, smirking. "Anyone who joins me will have an all-new kit."

She unzipped her bodysuit and Harvey heard his entire team gasp. She was wearing a golden shirt, dazzling silver shorts and socks, and — of course — Armadillos. Harvey couldn't take his eyes off them.

"Plus," Jackie continued, lifting one of her Imps to show off their gold-banded studs, "members of my team can choose anything else they need from my family's shop — for free."

There was a buzz of excitement around Harvey as if someone had stirred a beehive with a stick. Someone called eagerly to Jackie, "What's your team called?"

"We're The Superteam," Jackie replied. "Didn't you know? You're playing us next Saturday — if The Team still has any players left by then."

Chapter 3

"Look on the bright side," said Steffi. "Quality opposition means The Team will have to become better. It'll be good for us."

"But she wants to steal our players!" said Darren.

"And our name," said Harvey. "She's just putting 'super' in front of it, that's all."

"Jackie Spoyle might always get what she wants," said Rita, "but she's not having The Team!" She snatched the ball from Matt and angrily kicked it into the air.

There was a silence, followed by a loud gong that sounded like someone had hit a rubbish bin with a baseball bat. Harvey turned and saw Mark 1 rubbing his head as he bounded over, his eyes flashing.

The robot put a powerful hand on Harvey's shoulder, and began dragging him away. "Mine!" he bleated urgently. "MINE!"

Harvey jogged along beside Mark 1, trying not to catch his big toe in the grass, or slap it on the pavement. Darren and Rita followed behind.

"What's wrong?" Harvey kept asking, but Mark 1 didn't reply.

When they reached Baker Street, Harvey increased his pace. Something was going on at the inventing tower. As they drew closer he saw a sign:

"For Sale: Amazing Inventions!"

Professor Gertie lumbered from the tower door, her arms full of strange and wonderful-looking objects which she tipped with a crash onto her lawn.

Harvey heard Mark 1 start to tick rapidly, like a bomb about to go off.

"Have no fear!" Professor Gertie said when she spotted them. "By this time tomorrow, Harvey will be ankle-deep in Armadillos!"

Darren squatted down and grabbed an invention. It was the Shoosh! Gun that Harvey had seen Professor Gertie use to shoot nets over spiders. Rita poked delicately at some portable Lock Jaws, which were a new kind of safe.

"You won't have any problem selling these!" Darren said. "It's our first day back at school tomorrow and nearly everyone walks past here."

"Do they really?" Professor Gertie said, giving Harvey a knowing wink.

With a distressed *beep!*, Mark 1 let go of Harvey's arm, scooped up as many things as he could from the ground, and bounded inside the tower with them. Harvey heard him clattering up the stairs at top speed.

Professor Gertie sighed loudly. "For some reason, that robot thinks all my useless gadgets belong to him. His bedroom is packed full of them!"

"You mean this is all Mark 1's?" said Rita.

"Don't worry," said Professor Gertie. "There's nothing here of any real value."

Harvey couldn't believe what he was hearing. "I'm not having any boots bought with Mark 1's stuff!" he said, looking to Rita and Darren for support.

"It's totally unfair," agreed Rita. "But then again …" She bit her lip. "We won't beat The Superteam if you have to play in your socks, will we?"

"You're our captain," said Darren firmly. "If you can't play your best, The Team won't hold together. You need boots, Harvey."

"And I ruined your Armadillos," said Professor Gertie. "So you have to let me buy you another pair."

Harvey shook his head, but didn't say anything.

"To tell the truth," Professor Gertie said brightly, "I'm quite enjoying myself. It's about time my inventions earned me some cash!"

She skipped merrily back inside the tower.

"Mark 1 shouldn't have to suffer," Harvey told Darren and Rita. "If there was any other way of getting new boots, I'd take it."

"Well, there is one possibility," said Rita. "You could borrow Steffi's spare pair."

Darren was aghast. "But they're pink!"

Rita retreated down Baker Street, pulling Darren along with her.

"Pink boots are better than no boots," Rita insisted.

"Don't do it, Harvey!" Darren cried.

Darren was right, Harvey thought. There was no way his reputation would survive if he was seen wearing pink boots.

That night, Harvey stayed up late, watching through his bedroom window as Professor Gertie carried inventions from her tower, and Mark 1 bundled them straight back inside again. The robot was now making furious popping noises, and giving off steam.

Then, around ten o'clock, Harvey heard a high-pitched *BEEEEeeeeeeeeep*! followed by silence. Mark 1 didn't emerge from the tower again.

Harvey felt uneasy as he crawled into bed and began rubbing his sore toes. He didn't know what he was going to do. The Team needed him — but so did Mark 1.

As he drifted off to sleep, he was only sure of one thing — he would stand and face The Superteam on Saturday, even if he had to play barefoot. *Nobody* was going to take over The Team.

Chapter 4

A girl was shrieking, "I'm having it, and there's nothing you can do about it!"

Harvey's eyes flipped open. Darting to his window, he saw that it was morning, and Professor Gertie's Amazing Inventions sale was in full swing.

Harvey hurriedly searched for the trousers and jumper he'd worn to school last year, and tugged them on. Everything felt tight and short, and he couldn't even get his shoes on his feet until he had loosened the laces as far as they would go.

"One at a time!" he heard Professor Gertie holler. "If you fight over them, they'll be broken!"

Harvey left his house at a run and jumped over the fence into Professor Gertie's garden. He dodged a group of small boys who were stuck together with Velcro Balls, and spotted Professor Gertie sitting at a table facing a long queue of shoppers.

Harvey groaned. He was too late. Nearly all her inventions had gone already. He looked around for Mark 1, but couldn't see him.

A girl next to him held up a pile of paper. "What's this?" she asked.

"Aha," said Professor Gertie. "That's my Rub-a-Dub paper!"

Harvey watched her press a piece of the plain paper onto her open notebook. When she peeled it off, she'd made an exact copy.

"It's for homework!" the girl squealed. Professor Gertie began to sell the Rub-a-Dub paper a sheet at a time.

Darren arrived, looking pleased. "At this rate she'll have the money to buy your boots in no time," said Darren. "Come on — we're late."

As they walked down the hill, Harvey felt cool air around his wrists and ankles. He tried pulling his sleeves down, but they sprang back up again. Then, as they turned into the school grounds, he was met by a chorus of giggling girls. Jackie Spoyle was standing with her friends, blocking the path.

"Look everyone," said Jackie. "This year Harvey Boots is setting the style!"

Harvey blushed as Jackie's gang shrieked with laughter.

Darren barged through them, making a gap so that Harvey could follow.

"Steffi says Harvey *likes* old things," Jackie went on. "He doesn't look very comfortable in them, though!"

Darren rounded on her. "What have you been talking to Steffi for?"

"I've been chatting to all the league's stars," Jackie said primly. "I do wish Steffi went to our school. She's got the right kind of attitude, hasn't she? And Rita, too — she's *very* keen."

Darren's face turned fiery red, but before he could say anything else, Harvey hustled him into their classroom. "Forget about it," Harvey said. "Rita would never play for her."

Darren collapsed onto a chair at the back of the class. "Maybe not," he said. "But some of the others might. Steffi's always complaining that we don't have a trendy kit. She'll be the first to go."

Throughout the morning, Harvey and Darren tried to work out who would be tempted to join The Superteam. They had plenty of time to talk while their teacher, Mr Spottiwoode, tried to keep the class from rioting.

"I hope Professor Gertie doesn't get into trouble for this," Harvey said as a boy near them used the Shoosh! Gun to fire nets over himself until his hair looked like it was covered in thick, stringy cobwebs.

Darren was batting away bubbles. "Where are these coming from?" he said. One burst over him. "Hey — they stink!"

"It must be Professor Gertie's Blow Off," Harvey explained. "It captures smells inside bubbles. Rekha's using it."

By the end of the day, Mr Spottiwoode's desk was piled high with confiscated inventions, and Darren was busy scribbling a list of all the players The Team was likely to lose.

He showed it to Harvey on their way home.

"You've written down everyone but me and you!" said Harvey.

"We're the only ones I can be absolutely sure about," said Darren.

"What about Rita?"

Darren grimaced. "We can't be certain …"

"Yes we can," said Harvey, and he scratched out Rita's name. Then he noticed a large crowd gathered around Professor Gertie's tower.

"What's going on?" he said, breaking into a run. "I thought she sold everything this morning."

Darren jumped up to see over people's heads. "Looks like she's found a few tonnes more. Mark 1's bedroom must have been jam-packed!"

They pushed their way through, and found Professor Gertie weighing an ancient handbag in her hands. It made a dull rattle just like the sound Harvey's piggy bank had made when it was full.

Professor Gertie waved when she saw Harvey. "If I keep my sale going all week, we should have enough money for your boots by Friday."

"All week?" said Harvey dismally. "How many more inventions do you have left to sell?"

"*Thousands*," purred Professor Gertie, rubbing her hands together.

"How's Mark 1?" Harvey asked hopefully. "Is he feeling better?"

"He won't get out of bed," said Professor Gertie. "He normally only does that when he's thinking very hard, but this time he seems to have turned himself off!"

Harvey felt terrible. Mark 1 had never turned himself off before! Harvey had to tell Professor Gertie to stop the sale. There was no way he could accept boots bought in this way.

"I'm not —" he started to say, and then he was knocked off his feet as a crush of shoppers suddenly surged forwards. He just had time to see someone holding up a thing that looked like a builder's hat with helicopter blades before he crawled away on his hands and knees.

"I've got an idea," Darren said excitedly as Harvey stood up. "The Team's training sessions are always on a Thursday night, right?"

"Yeah," sighed Harvey. "So what?"

"So, the people who turn up on Thursday will see that The Team's captain still hasn't got boots, and they might decide to join Spoyle's team after all."

"There's nothing we can do about it," said Harvey.

"There is," said Darren. "I'll call everyone and change the training session to Friday." He grinned. "When they see your Armadillos, there's no way they'll give up on The Team!"

As he watched Darren jog home, Harvey felt his own energy drain away. He slouched into his house and up to his room.

"I'm not going to wear Professor Gertie's Armadillos," he decided finally.

There had to be some other way of keeping The Team together. Harvey curled up in bed and began to think very hard.

He was soon snoring noisily.

Chapter 5

The rest of the week seemed to Harvey like a game everyone else was playing while he sat on the sidelines and watched.

On Wednesday, Professor Gertie's sale was busier than the day before, Jackie and her friends welcomed him to school with a well-practised cheer, Darren talked constantly about the new Armadillos Harvey would be getting, and Mr Spottiwoode spent the whole day pouncing on Professor Gertie's inventions.

On Thursday morning, the sale was still busy, Jackie and her friends applauded Harvey when he arrived at school, and Mr Spottiwoode lost part of his moustache when a hungry Frizz Bee landed on his nose.

"They're for trimming knotted bits of hair, actually," Harvey heard Rekha explain to her friend. "Definitely *not* moustaches."

Harvey's spirits rose briefly on Thursday

afternoon. He scored with one of his best-ever swerving free kicks in the playground — and Jackie Spoyle was watching.

"That will give her something to think about!" Darren shouted, adding to Harvey, "You'll be unstoppable — when you've got your Armadillos."

At last, on Friday morning, Harvey began to feel some relief. Professor Gertie, who looked exhausted, was no longer bringing out more inventions from her tower. And when Harvey got to school, Jackie and her friends were nowhere in sight.

"When Spoyle saw you score yesterday, she got worried," Darren reported later that afternoon. "She's now promising The Superteam free tickets to professional games, a real football coach, *and* an all-expenses-paid international summer tournament!"

Harvey felt like he'd been kicked in the stomach. "How can we compete with that?" he said despairingly.

"Easy," said Darren. "First, you get your Armadillos. That will help most of The Team decide to stay with us. Then we hammer The Superteam into the ground."

Harvey saw a triumphant glint in Darren's eyes, and knew he was going to let his friend down badly. He wouldn't be wearing Armadillos, and it was about time he told Darren.

Suddenly, Harvey heard a long, agonised scream, and saw Paul Pepper waving his hand violently in the air, trying to dislodge a pair of Lock Jaws.

"What on earth *is* that?" demanded Mr Spottiwoode.

"I keep my pencils in it," said the shy boy who sat next to Paul Pepper. He keyed a code into the base of the Lock Jaw, and Paul Pepper's hand was released. "I bought it from the professor who lives next door to Harvey Boots," the boy said. "That's where *all* the weird things came from."

The bell began to clang for the end of the day, and Harvey and Darren ducked their heads and bolted from the room. "Let's get the money, then go to Spoyle's to buy your Armadillos," urged Darren.

They ran through the school gates and into Baker Street where Harvey tugged on Darren's arm to make him stop. "I can't do it," he said. "The money belongs to Mark 1, and he should have it."

Harvey looked into his friend's face, expecting Darren to be devastated — or at least upset. But to his surprise, Darren smiled with satisfaction.

"Brilliant idea!" he said, blinking rapidly as he worked it out. "Mark 1 gets the cash, and then we ask him to do what he was invented for: saving The Team."

Harvey was confused. Had Darren forgotten? "The refs won't let robots play," Harvey reminded him.

Darren shook his head. "I didn't mean that. All Mark 1 has to do is buy you some Armadillos!"

Harvey thought about it, and began to feel excited. Of course Mark 1 would want to help them! "Let Mark 1 choose what to do,"

Harvey decided. "If he wants to get me some boots, I'll wear them. But I'll pay him back. I don't care how long it takes. I could even buy back some of Professor Gertie's inventions for him …"

Darren sneezed. "What's that smell?"

Harvey sniffed, and the memory of melting Armadillos came back to him like a nightmare he couldn't forget. He glanced up and saw a wisp of smoke rising from beside the inventing tower.

They found Professor Gertie standing in her garden, as still as a statue, holding the plant sprayer with the skull-and-crossbones stickers. On the path next to her, a pair of Armadillo Aces was on fire.

"I made it fresh," she said weakly, giving the sprayer a tiny shake. "I decided to buy your boots for you as a surprise, and I was rushing to have them ready and — oh, Harvey, I must have made a mistake when I mixed the formula up!"

"Not again!" said Darren. "Wait a minute — how much of the money did you spend?"

"*All* of it!" whimpered Professor Gertie.

"There's nothing else we can do, then," said Darren, holding his head in his hands. "I give up!"

Chapter 6

Harvey and Darren met Rita on the pitch that night. While they waited for the others to arrive, Darren told her about the new Armadillos.

"I know that Professor Gertie means well," Rita said, speaking very, very quietly. "But sometimes," she said, her voice rising, "I wish she would stop trying to MAKE THINGS BETTER!"

"Me too," said Harvey.

"Me three," said Darren grumpily.

"And where *is* everyone?" Rita snapped, when it was clear that nobody else was going to turn up. "I thought Matt would be with us, at least."

"You did tell everyone that the training session had changed to tonight, didn't you?" Harvey checked with Darren.

Darren slapped his forehead with his gloved hand.

"You mean you didn't?!" cried Rita. "But hang on — you told *me*!"

"I was too busy persuading the others not to join The Superteam!" said Darren. "I just forgot!"

"But that means that anyone else who wanted to stay on The Team would have turned up *yesterday*!" cried Rita.

"And because we weren't there," said Harvey, "they'll think we've joined Jackie's team. So they'll probably all join too!"

Friday night training was over.

It was dark when Harvey arrived home. Someone was waiting outside his house.

"Here's what you need," said Jackie Spoyle.

Harvey could barely see what she was giving him, but he knew the feel of Armadillos as he held them in his hands. And these weren't Aces. They were lighter, and more supple, and —

"They're your size," said Jackie. "I'm captain of The Superteam — but tomorrow, you can be our striker."

Harvey didn't hear her leave. He was busy getting used to his Imps.

Chapter 7

Harvey left his house on a cloudy Saturday morning carrying a shopping bag.

"You were right and I was wrong," said Professor Gertie, who was trying to fix her trampled flowerbeds. "I should never have taken away Mark 1's things. He won't come out of his room, or let me in — and I *know* he's up to something in there."

"You did what you thought was best," said Harvey.

Professor Gertie wasn't listening to him. "I wish I could give his toys back, but there was only one thing that I didn't sell." She pointed to a shadow behind the tower door. Harvey took a step closer to see what was there, then cringed as icy goosebumps ran up and down his spine.

It was Masher, the monstrous waste-disposal machine that Professor Gertie had made to eat inventions that didn't work.

Harvey once had a nightmare that Masher was trying to catch him. Now, looking into the killer machine's beady eyes, he wondered if he really had been dreaming. Its rows of jagged teeth were gnawing on the chain that secured it to a metal ring on the wall, and its crab-like claw was nipping chunks out of a sign that said:

Weird Pet For Sale! (Pat him — he's friendly!)

"Y-you've got to be joking!" spluttered Harvey.

"People are always on the look out for something different," said Professor Gertie. "And Masher would make an ideal family companion. He likes children, he only needs oiling once a week, and he eats any old junk."

Harvey eyed Masher warily, as he would a dog that was known to bite. A noise like stones being crushed came from deep inside the creature's mechanical jaws.

"His growl is worse than his bite," said Professor Gertie. "His teeth are worn down, and his claw is blunt, the poor dear."

Harvey was about to tell Professor Gertie that she couldn't let Masher loose on innocent people, when he realised he had nothing to worry about. There was *no way* anybody would want Masher.

"I have to go," said Harvey. "And don't worry about my boots anymore — I'm sorted."

When he reached the field, Harvey saw The Team mingling with about twenty other players. He recognised most of them — they were nearly all the league's best goal scorers.

Jackie hadn't picked a single defender, and Harvey guessed that The Superteam's defence was going to be useless.

He spotted Jackie modelling The Superteam's gold and silver uniform. Behind her there was a neat pile of Armadillo cases. The Superteam players were going to be equipped with the finest, just as Jackie had promised.

Harvey strolled up to her.

"Hi, Striker," said Jackie. "I'm glad you're with us." She unfolded a golden shirt and draped it over his shoulders. "This is for you," she said, beaming.

Harvey lifted the Imps from his bag. He saw Darren and Rita standing side by side, with their mouths open in disbelief.

"No thanks," Harvey said to Jackie. "I have a team already. These are for you."

Jackie's smile vanished as he gave her back the Imps. She snatched back the shirt.

"You *lose*, Harvey Boots," she spat after him as he turned his back on her. "You've already *lost*."

Harvey, Darren and Rita headed arm-in-arm towards the pitch. Harvey's heart was thumping. This was it. If the rest of The Team didn't follow, he really would have lost before the game had even started.

Steffi strode past them. "Come on," she said angrily, "let's show Superbrat what a *real* team can do!"

Matt trotted closely behind her. "Poor Steffi!" he said loudly. "She wasn't part of Spoilt's designs — she was only asked to be their *substitute*!"

Harvey watched with pride as The Team took their positions on the field.

"I don't get it," said Darren. "They're *all* here!"

"Of course they are," said Rita. "We're The Team, remember? Teams are teams because they stick together, no matter what."

Harvey, though, noticed that some of his team mates were frowning at his well-worn school shoes.

"These are fine," he told everyone. "I play in them every day."

"On grass?" said Steffi.

"No," said Harvey, "but —"

"In the wet?" said Steffi as a dark cloud bathed them in shadow.

Harvey didn't answer her. "If it rains," he muttered to Rita, "my shoes are going to slide all over the place."

"It won't rain," Rita said confidently.

The teams faced each other. The Superteam squad who weren't playing this time stood on the sidelines, wearing golden baseball caps and chanting their support.

The ref blew her whistle and Harvey kicked off, just as a cold drop landed on his nose.

"That cloud hasn't got more than an eggcup of rain in it," said Rita carelessly as she returned the ball to him.

Heavy drops began pattering on Harvey's head. He back-heeled the ball to Steffi, then ran into space to receive it. But as he reached

out his left leg, his right foot slipped, tumbling him to the grass. Rita gathered the ball and headed for The Superteam goal. Harvey could hardly see her through the downpour, and the next thing he knew a Superteam player was trying to set up an attack.

Harvey closed in on her fast, stuck out his foot to intercept the ball, then skidded, tripped and dived headfirst into her stomach, knocking her flat on her back.

The ref stood over Harvey, showing him a yellow card. "Outrageous foul!" she said furiously. "One more like that and I'm sending you off!"

Harvey slipped over twice more as he limped to the side of the field. The shower was stopping, but the grass was already soaked and muddy.

"Keep out of the action until it dries," Rita advised him.

Harvey watched helplessly as the game went on in front of him. His absence was putting The Team under pressure, but Harvey was encouraged by how they responded.

Rita dropped back into defence, and they built their forward moves slowly so that The Superteam couldn't break through them on the counterattack. The problem was, The Team were unable to finish their attacks; without Harvey, they didn't have a natural goal-scorer — but The Superteam had plenty.

Harvey watched Paul Pepper gather the ball and set a straight course for Darren's goal, skipping past one Team player after another.

"Tackle him!" Harvey bellowed. Matt, Steffi and Rita lunged for the ball, but Paul Pepper still managed to shoot.

Darren dived at full stretch, pushed the ball onto the post with his fingertips, and slid along the grass, leaving the goal undefended. Harvey put up his arms to celebrate the save — and then saw Jackie trot up to the ball. All she had to do was walk it into the net. With a grin of triumph on her face, she did.

Harvey watched in frustration as Jackie Spoyle did a victory dance in front of him. He felt desperate. He had to play … somehow.

Then he saw Mark 1 pelting across the field, balancing a tattered picnic hamper on his head and calling urgently, "Boo-oootz!"

Chapter 8

The robot set the hamper on the ground, and Harvey rummaged among a jumbled mass of string, a sink plunger, yoghurt tubs with smiley faces painted on the sides, old corks, a tea strainer, and two egg cartons packed with grey powder.

"Is there something here for me?" Harvey asked.

"Boo-ootz!" said the robot, nodding happily.

Harvey searched again. He heard The Superteam cheer as they scored a second goal, and he began to panic. "Where are they?" he said anxiously. "Which boots?"

Mark 1 bent down and unravelled the strung-together objects. Then he wrapped them around Harvey's shoes. He pulled the strings tight, tied a complicated knot, and held Harvey's hand as he tried to balance on the wobbly egg cartons.

Harvey didn't know what to say. The Superteam were celebrating their third goal, and he was standing on rubbish.

He took a step. After all, he told himself, Mark 1 had made them for him. The least he could do was *try* them.

Mark 1 shoved him onto the field just as the ball came bouncing their way.

Harvey took huge strides towards it. Concentrating on not falling over, he didn't hear the whistle for half-time. Instead, he lined himself up to kick the ball, drew back his left foot, and —

The egg cartons exploded.

"Aaargh!" cried Harvey as he flew into the air, flapped his arms wildly, and crashed to the ground.

The Team wandered over as Harvey kicked off his burning shoes and Mark 1 snatched them up, tutting as he examined them.

"Looks like I'm playing in my bare feet," said Harvey as he quickly rolled off his smouldering socks.

A pair of pink Primadonnas fell into his lap. He looked up to see Steffi's embarrassed but determined face. "It's our only chance," she said.

Harvey heard The Superteam and their supporters start chanting, "Boot up, boot up, Har-vey Boots!" Jackie was laughing so hard her teeth reminded him of Professor Gertie's Lock Jaws.

"Don't even think about it," Darren warned him, pointing at Steffi's boots as if he was telling them off. "Just — don't."

But Harvey knew it was their only hope. He put them on, stood up — and saw Professor Gertie marching towards him, holding a Spoyle Sports' shoe box.

"No!" Harvey exclaimed, feeling like everything around him was going wrong, wrong, wrong. "You can't have sold Masher!"

"Even better than that," said Professor Gertie.

"But he's *dangerous*!" Harvey roared.

"Mr Spotty? Oh, I wouldn't say he was *that* bad," said Professor Gertie in surprise.

"Mr Spotty?" Harvey said, bewildered.

"Your *teacher*," explained Professor Gertie.

"Mr Spottiwoode bought Masher?" said Darren.

"Of course he didn't," said Professor Gertie. "He came to ask about my inventions."

"Are you in trouble?" Harvey said seriously.

"Quite the opposite," said Professor Gertie. "Your wonderful Mr Spotty wants to buy thirty Lock Jaws!"

"What does he want those for?" said Darren.

"He wants everyone in his class to have a secure pencil case," said the professor. "Mr Spotty said he'll be able to start his lessons on time if he doesn't have to find all the lost pencils and pens first."

"And he *paid* you for them?" said Darren in astonishment.

"Yes!" cried Professor Gertie delightedly. "Actually," she said, "he only gave me a little bit to start with, and it wasn't enough to buy the boots you wanted, Harvey. I could only afford the cheapest pair."

"*Any* will do," said Harvey with relief as Professor Gertie handed him a pair of ordinary black boots.

"Don't worry," the professor said, leaning close so that only Harvey could hear.

"I stopped by the tower on the way here to spice them up a bit."

Harvey groaned and hung his head, wishing that just for once Professor Gertie wouldn't interfere. Everything she'd invented for him lately had been a disaster.

"Aren't you going to try them?" she said.

Harvey shrugged. He put on the new boots carefully, handed Steffi back her Primadonnas, and walked to the edge of the centre circle, taking small, delicate steps.

His feet felt cool and airy. Without thinking, he bounced up and down to get ready — then stopped. His toes had begun to tingle.

"Are you all right?" said Rita. "You look scared!"

Harvey didn't reply. He heard the ref blow her whistle to start the second half, and felt his body tensing up expectantly. He had no idea what would happen next.

Chapter 9

The Superteam kicked off and Rita chased for the ball. Harvey didn't move. His feet had suddenly become warm.

"Move it, Harvey!" called Matt, threading the ball to him. Harvey automatically took a step forward and intercepted it, feeling his boots respond like ordinary boots should. The only difference was that these were so snug they felt like his feet's second skin.

Harvey was too nervous to kick the ball, so he used the side of his foot to roll it back to Steffi — and was surprised to note that it arrived exactly where he'd intended. Seeing a gap, he burst through, collected the ball on the run and stroked it gently ahead of him. Now he had a chance for a long shot.

"Shoot!" yelled Professor Gertie.

Harvey slowed down, waiting for his boots to do something they shouldn't. What *had* Professor Gertie done to them?

He nudged the ball again. Nothing happened. The Superteam defenders were closing in, but he still had time to shoot. If only he could believe that Professor Gertie's inventions didn't *always* catch fire or blow up or melt or just not work.

But some of the time her ideas did work …

"SHOOOOT!" insisted Mark 1.

With a mighty yell, Harvey put all his trust in Professor Gertie. He blasted the ball towards The Superteam goal, watching it take off like a missile, skimming the grass, and spinning to the left. The goalkeeper dived low and got both hands to it — but he couldn't stop it.

"Goal!"

As the rest of The Team and their two supporters celebrated, Harvey took a close look at his left boot. It still looked normal. "I don't believe it," he said, confused.

"Neither do I," said the ref suspiciously, pressing Harvey's boot with her thumbs. "You haven't got a lump of steel in here, have you?"

"I dunno," said Harvey. "I mean, no, they're not heavy."

The ref examined his other boot before restarting the game.

They felt alive, a part of him that did whatever he wanted them to do. He couldn't imagine what Professor Gertie had done to them, but he was sure of one thing — this time, her invention was a spectacular success.

Harvey sailed in a cross, and Rita thundered the ball into the net with her head. Goal!

Harvey's back flip fooled The Superteam defence, leaving the way open for Matt to trickle the ball home. Goal!

Harvey sent the ball curling from a free kick for his second goal, and soon after made his hat-trick directly from a corner kick. Goal! Goal!

"Am I dreaming?" said Darren, snatching off a glove so he could pinch himself.

"This is pathetic!" Harvey heard Paul Pepper whine as Steffi headed the ball through the goalie's legs. "Call this a superteam? We might as well give up."

Other players from Jackie's team nodded their heads in agreement.

"Play on!" Jackie ordered. "I say when we give up!"

Harvey put his foot on the ball and watched as Paul Pepper wrenched off his top and threw it at her. "I don't like your style!" he hollered. "This isn't a team at all!"

"I know it's a bit early," said the ref hurriedly, "but we might as well call it a day." She blew the final whistle and said, "The Team win six to three!"

Harvey tore down the field with his arms in the air — and saw Darren staring at him with a look of terror on his face.

"What's wro—" Harvey began, and then he heard a sound of grinding metal behind him. He spun around.

Masher's feet were pounding deep holes in the grass as it came at Harvey, teeth whizzing like chainsaws, claw snapping, and bitten-through chain whipping the air.

Harvey dived out of the way, rolled onto his knees, and looked about. Masher continued past him across the field, with Professor Gertie trailing behind.

"Mashy!" she cooed gently. "Here, Mashy!"

Masher reached The Superteam, its eyes rocking back and forth as if looking for someone. Harvey heard Paul Pepper bellow, "Your Superteam are JUNK!"

Suddenly, Masher darted forward. Jackie screamed as the metal monster pinched off one of her Armadillo Imps with his claw. Still screaming, she sprinted across the field.

Rita giggled. "Looks like Mashy's got the munchies!"

"But why did he pick on Spoyle?" said Darren.

"Because," laughed Harvey, "he eats any old junk!"

Professor Gertie dashed after Masher and pulled him back by his chain. Then she gave Mark 1 a one-armed hug.

"That means sorry," she said. "From now on, anything I make that doesn't work is yours forever."

"He'll need an aircraft hanger to store it all," said Darren under his breath.

Professor Gertie put Masher's chain into Mark 1's hand and said, "How would you like a weird pet?"

The robot's eyes flickered as he bent down to stroke the wire bristles on Masher's back. Masher made a purring noise, and Harvey covered his ears. The sound was horrible.

"Professor Gertie, *what* did you do to Harvey's boots?" Rita wanted to know. "I mean, they were fantastic!"

"*Harvey* was fantastic," said Professor Gertie, prising off Harvey's left boot. "All I did was … this!" She pulled out a long plug of

cotton wool. "They didn't have these boots in Harvey's size," she explained, "so I had to stuff the toes to make them fit."

Harvey gasped. "Is that *all*? I thought —"

Professor Gertie smiled. "You didn't think I was going to let you down, did you?" she said innocently.

Harvey looked around. Darren and Rita were always with him, of course. But so were the rest of The Team — and that included Mark 1 and Professor Gertie. They stuck together, no matter what.

Harvey grinned at Professor Gertie. "You? Let me down?" He started to laugh. "Never!"

BANNED!

Chapter 1

"It's on!" whispered Harvey as Darren, who had just arrived at school, sat down next to him.

Darren ducked behind a large book with a picture of a rocket on the front, and said, "What is?"

Harvey glanced towards the front of the classroom, where Mr Spottiwoode, their teacher, was standing, his mouth moving lazily under his moustache as he began writing Tuesday's work on the board.

Harvey said excitedly in Darren's ear, "The Floodlights Cup!"

"The *what*?!" Darren said loudly, sitting straight up.

"Sshhh!" hissed Harvey, dragging him down again and looking anxiously towards Mr Spottiwoode, who was now blowing his nose noisily. Harvey watched him tuck his hanky back inside his pocket, then begin talking. It sounded like his usual speech — something about trying harder and doing better. Harvey turned back to Darren and said, "You know how they're putting floodlights on our pitch this week?"

"Yeah," said Darren eagerly, nodding for Harvey to go on.

"Well," said Harvey, "to celebrate, there's going to be an evening match."

Darren's eyes widened.

"And," Harvey continued, "the winners get a silver Floodlights Cup!"

Darren's eyes nearly popped out of his skull. "A silver cup!"

Harvey knew exactly how Darren was feeling. The Team had never won a cup before. They had only received a certificate for coming top of the league last season.

"Rita told me about it last night," Harvey explained. "Her dad is helping to organise it. There's a big cup that The Team holds for a year, with our name engraved on it, and medals for each of us to keep. If we win, that is."

"We will," said Darren determinedly. "Who are we playing?"

Harvey smoothed out a piece of paper. "I wrote it down," he said, showing it to Darren.

"Finbar Fly's All Stars," read Darren in a puzzled voice. "Who are they?"

"Never heard of them," said Harvey, grinning.

"Finbar Fly!" snorted Darren. "They sound second rate. No, *third* rate." He turned to face Harvey. "Looks like The Team are finally going to win a cup!"

Harvey nodded happily. A team they'd never even heard of wasn't likely to be a problem.

"When do we get our silverware?" said Darren.

"Saturday night," said Harvey. "After the game."

Darren spent the rest of Tuesday asking Harvey questions. How big were the medals? Was the cup completely silver, or was there some gold in it, too? And would all their names be engraved on it, or just "The Team"?

Harvey did his best to answer. They could talk easily that afternoon because their teacher had taken them into the playground to pull on a giant elastic band. Mr Spottiwoode held on to one end, and one by one the class pulled on the other end.

"Why are we doing this?" asked Darren, straining, when it was his turn.

"Dunno," said Harvey.

Back in the classroom, Harvey hurriedly packed up, and as soon as the bell went he pushed towards the door.

"Mr Boots!"

Harvey swivelled around. His teacher was beckoning him over.

As Harvey made his way to Mr Spottiwoode's desk, he noticed that everyone else was clutching a white envelope. Darren was eyeing his worriedly.

"Do you even know what these are about?" Mr Spottiwoode asked him sternly.

"Er, of course," said Harvey. "I mean, no. Sorry."

"I've told the class about a dozen times!" Mr Spottiwoode pursed his lips and his moustache stood out like a tiny umbrella.

"Oh, yeah. That. Now I remember," said Harvey, trying to sound convincing.

Mr Spottiwoode sighed as he handed Harvey an envelope. *For the Attention of Mr and Mrs Boots*, read Harvey.

"Uh, thanks," he said.

Together, he and Darren headed for the school gate. Darren was already tearing paper.

"Is that for you?" said Harvey, surprised.

"It's for my folks," admitted Darren. "But I always read my reports first, so I can warn them."

"Reports?" said Harvey. He read over Darren's shoulder, "Mid-term Report".

Underneath there was a list of the topics they'd been studying in class, followed by comments from Mr Spottiwoode. Every one of the comments was, "Satisfactory".

"Phew!" said Darren with relief. "That *is* satisfying! Go on, Harvey, open yours. *You* haven't got anything to worry about — your report is always better than mine."

Harvey opened his envelope carefully so that he could seal it again. Then he gasped.

Next to every topic, Mr Spottiwoode had scrawled the same word in thick black ink. "*Failing*." But it was what his teacher had written at the bottom of the page that really set Harvey's heart pounding.

"Harvey's normally high standards have taken a dive. He **must** concentrate in lessons! I recommend that he be banned from playing football until his school work improves.

Yours sincerely,

F. Spottiwoode."

Harvey could hardly breathe. He felt as if he'd just been winded by a crunching tackle. Silently, he handed his report to Darren.

Darren's mouth dropped open. "What about the Floodlights Cup?"

Harvey felt a lump rising in his throat.

"Harvey," cried Darren, "you can't play. You're *banned*!"

Chapter 2

Harvey walked up Baker Street in a daze, hardly aware that Darren was following him. He wished he didn't have to go home. He knew that as soon as his mum and dad read his report they'd do exactly what Mr Spottiwoode had recommended. He'd be banned from playing for The Team.

"I know that I talk a lot," said Darren apologetically. "I can't help it. But we do still listen sometimes, don't we?"

"You do," said Harvey, morosely. The truth was, he'd been dreaming up some new moves for The Team, and when he wasn't listening to Darren, he liked to run through the moves in his head and imagine how they'd turn out. "I've been daydreaming," he admitted. "It's my own fault."

Harvey ground to a halt beside the gate to Professor Gertie's inventing tower. He heard a whirring noise, and looked up.

Professor Gertie, who was Harvey's next-door neighbour, was dangling from a rope halfway up the tower. She seemed to be riding

a bike, knitting, *and* trying to clean a window with a sponge the size of a dinner table.

"Yoo-hoo!" she called, pedalling madly as she coasted to the ground. The wheels skidded on the grass and Professor Gertie slipped off the bike, landing with a *sploosh*! on the soapy sponge.

When she stood up, she was soaked from head to foot with dirty water.

"Nice, er, whatever it is!" Harvey heard Rita call from behind him and Darren. She was panting, and Harvey guessed she'd run all the way from her school.

"For your information," Professor Gertie told Rita, "that's my latest invention: a Chore All. I can use it to do my two least favourite jobs at once — cleaning dirty windows and de-holing socks."

"What's the bicycle for?" asked Darren curiously.

"Pedalling provides the lifting force, of course!" Professor Gertie said briskly, as if that part was obvious. Harvey had no idea what she was talking about.

"Now then," Professor Gertie said, noticing Harvey's glum expression. "What's up with you?"

Without a word, Harvey handed her his report, and she and Rita read it together.

Professor Gertie's face turned the colour of beetroot. "Rats on fire!" she fumed. "Can teachers really do that?"

"Not at my school," said Rita. "The worst grade they give is a W."

"A what?" said Darren.

"It stands for 'Worrying'. They don't say 'Failing' because it might make a person feel useless."

Harvey shrugged. "I don't care what word they use," he said. "If I'm rubbish, I'd rather be told about it."

"We'll have to pull out of the Finbar game," said Darren. Harvey could tell he was trying to hide his disappointment.

"What's a Finbar game?" asked Professor Gertie.

Harvey and Rita quickly explained about the Floodlights Cup.

"It's only a silver cup anyway," Darren said. "There's probably no gold in it."

"The Team can still play," Harvey insisted. "I'm the only one who's banned — no one else should have to miss out."

"But you're our captain!" said Rita, shocked. "The Team needs you!"

"Of course Harvey will play!" snapped Professor Gertie. "I'll find a way, have no fear about that!" Holding Harvey's report in the air, she declared firmly, "Harvey — you're playing!"

Harvey waited hopefully for something to happen, but nothing did.

"How can I?" he said at last.

Suddenly Mark 1, the Football Machine, jumped out of the window of the inventing tower, and landed lightly behind Professor Gertie on his Bouncing Boots. He was her greatest invention, a robot designed purely for football.

"Playyy?" the robot said eagerly in his strange, mechanical voice.

"Not now," Professor Gertie told him impatiently. "I'm trying to think. Anyway," she said, as the smell of pizza filled the air, "it's time for your dinner."

Mark 1's laser eyes flashed red. The robot's head swivelled, his neck stretched, and he opened his mouth.

"Hey!" said Harvey. "Hang on — she didn't mean—"

The metal jaws closed on Harvey's report and tugged it from Professor Gertie's hand.

"Stop!" cried Harvey.

Mark 1 began to chew.

"Spit it out!" said Professor Gertie crossly, taking hold of Mark 1's head and feeling around inside his mouth. "Ouch!" she yelped. "He bit me!"

Mark 1 beeped, and began to swallow. Harvey watched a shape like a ping-pong ball moving down his throat.

Mark 1 burped.

"Where's my report?" said Harvey weakly.

No one answered.

"Oh no!" Professor Gertie suddenly dashed towards the tower door as black smoke began to billow from her kitchen window. "My pepperoni!"

Mark 1 bounced along behind her, beeping like a fire alarm.

Harvey, Rita and Darren followed the robot into Professor Gertie's tower. At the top of the twisting stairway, Harvey noticed that Darren was bent over, holding his stomach. At first Harvey thought he was being sick, but then he realised that Darren was laughing as if he'd just seen the funniest thing in the world.

"That robot!" Darren spluttered. "He's a genius! Now you *can't* show your report to your parents!"

"I know that!" said Harvey angrily. He was beginning to panic. "I'm going to be in even more trouble!"

"No you're not," said Darren. "Think about it, Harvey. This means you're only banned from playing football at school, where Mr Spottiwoode can check on you. But there's nothing to stop you playing after school!"

Harvey paused, thinking. He couldn't exactly show the report to his mum and dad now, could he? So he wouldn't be doing anything wrong. Not really.

Harvey felt excitement surge inside him. "Call an extra training session," he told Darren. "The Team are going to be well prepared for the Floodlights Cup."

"We'll have to be," said Rita quietly.

"Why?" said Darren.

"I've found out who Finbar Fly is — that's what I came to tell you." Harvey saw an agonised look pass over Rita's face. "Harvey, Darren — he's your *teacher*."

Chapter 3

"Mr Spottiwoode?" Darren began to cackle. "He's got hands like shovels and feet like a duck! And he's *old* — he must be thirty at least! Spot's All Stars — we'll slaughter them!"

Harvey wasn't smiling, though. He was still watching Rita, who looked deadly serious.

"He's the goalie," Rita said.

Darren looked at her.

"I guess his big hands and feet help him stop the ball," Rita mused. "My dad said he was a legend. The first professional player to come from our town. *And* he's the only goalie ever to have a one hundred percent clean sheet."

"He never let in a single goal?" said Harvey, awestruck.

"That's impossible," Darren said.

"He only played for one season," Rita explained. "Then he quit to become a teacher."

"He gave up being the best goalie ever for that?" said Darren in disbelief. "That can't be right."

"Maybe he was permanently injured," suggested Harvey.

"My dad said he just wanted to be a teacher more than anything else," said Rita. Then her eyes widened. "Hang on!" she said. "Harvey can't play in the Floodlights after all. Mr Spot is the one who banned him!"

"Oh no!" said Darren, putting his hands to his head.

Harvey was stunned.

"He must have been watching you score goals in the playground," said Darren hotly. "He realised you were going to ruin his precious goalkeeping record. That's why he wants you out of the game."

Harvey shook his head doubtfully. "I'm not that good," he said.

"And I don't think a teacher would do that," said Rita reasonably.

"Well this one would," Darren said grimly. "The test proves everything."

"Test?" said Harvey. "What test?"

Darren was amazed. "Don't you listen to *anything* Mr Spot says? On Friday morning we're being tested on every topic we've done this term."

"A test on everything!" said Rita in wonder. "That *is* mean."

Harvey felt his shoulders drooping. First he was banned from playing football, and now he had to do a test he could never pass.

Rita looked upset. "What if you study really hard?" she suggested. "Maybe you can do well enough in the test to make your teacher lift the ban."

"Yeah, maybe," said Harvey, trying to sound encouraging.

Darren shook his head gloomily. "Harvey will need to get top marks for Mr Spot to lift the ban," he said. "Let's face it — Finbar Fly's stolen our cup. It's over."

When Harvey left for school on Wednesday morning, there were bags under his eyes and he was yawning. He'd found a geography book beneath his bed, and stayed up late reading. But now, he couldn't remember a single thing about it.

As he walked past Professor Gertie's tower, he spotted a work table at the far end of the garden … With a cry of alarm, he sprinted over.

"What's wrong?" he shouted. "Has there been an accident?"

Mark 1 was lying on the table. Wires were pilling from his shirt like spaghetti, and his head looked like it had been cut off at the mouth.

"Don't worry," said Professor Gertie soothingly. "He's okay." She pressed the button on the robot's chest and he sat up.

Harvey flinched. The top part of Mark 1's head, which had been made from an old flip-top rubbish bin, was dangling down his back, connected by a hinge.

"I'm just doing some much-needed spring cleaning," said Professor Gertie brightly, swinging Mark 1's head back into place with a *click!*

"Hell-lo Harvvv," said the robot, rubbing his chin. Harvey winced as Professor Gertie lifted the lever above Mark 1's eyes and let his head fall back again. *Bonk!*

"Doesn't that hurt?" he said to the upside-down face. Talking to the headless robot made Harvey feel dizzy.

"Itt ticklezz!" said Mark 1 before Professor Gertie detached his head and carried it away.

"How are you, Harvey?" said Professor Gertie, concerned. "Did you sort out your problems with Mr Spotty?"

"I've got to pass a test," said Harvey.

"That won't be a problem for you!" said Professor Gertie confidently.

"There's a lot to learn, though," said Harvey. "And I've only got two days."

Professor Gertie just winked at him. "Forty-eight hours is plenty of time. Believe me, Harvey, you'll be fine. Between you and me," she said, lowering her voice and walking Harvey a few paces from the robot, "you're even a match for Mark 1, you know. Your passing is almost perfect, your goal-scoring is excellent, and your tactics are more clever than you realise. Harvey, you're a *leader*."

"But that's *football*," said Harvey. "Our test is on everything we do at *school*."

"I have complete faith in you, Harvey," said the professor absently. She bent over and began to poke inside Mark 1's rubbish-bin skull. She picked out an old bird's nest. "No wonder he's getting woolly-headed! Honestly, Harvey — Mark 1 may be the most brilliant robot ever invented, but he can't even remember to tie his bootlaces. Apart from coaching The Team, he doesn't do a single useful thing. And he eats *anything*!"

She pulled out a tangle of fishing line, a handful of sparkly sweet wrappers, and four marbles.

Harvey saw something else. Reaching in carefully, he squeezed it between his finger and thumb and tugged it free. It was covered with fluff.

"You missed this," he said. "I think it's a dried pea."

"Not quite," said the professor. "That's a Pea *Brain*!"

Harvey nearly dropped it. "It's a *what*?"

"It's Mark 1's control centre." Professor Gertie took the Pea Brain from Harvey, blew it clean, and put it back into Harvey's hand.

Harvey held it up to his eyes and saw tiny wires, as fine as hairs, sticking out of it.

"Is this all Mark 1 needs?" said Harvey. "To play football and everything?"

Professor Gertie nodded proudly.

But Harvey was not impressed. If it only took a brain the size of a pea to be a football genius, what did Harvey have inside his own head?

I bet I've got a Pea Brain too, he told himself miserably. And it won't be much use for a test on every topic in two days' time.

"I'd better get to school," he told Professor Gertie with a sigh. "I've got a *lot* of work to do."

Chapter 4

Harvey spent all Wednesday morning trying to read a history book, while Mr Spottiwoode droned on from the front of the classroom, and Darren talked furiously in his ear.

"Why is he called 'Fly' anyway?" Darren was saying. "He hasn't got six legs, or wings, and he doesn't buzz except when he's blowing his nose."

Harvey shrugged.

"And what's so special about a fly?" Darren went on. "A fly wouldn't be any good in goal. Its wings would get tangled in the net."

"There must be some reason ..." Harvey said as they watched Mr Spottiwoode move slowly around the room with his hands in his pockets. Harvey couldn't imagine him as a professional goalkeeper.

At lunchtime, Harvey had some bad news for Darren. "I'm staying here," he said, piling all his books onto his desk. "I have to study. I've got to try to learn something."

Darren blinked. "Okay," he said. "Me too."

"You don't have to," said Harvey. "You can play a match outside — you're not banned."

"I need to swot as well," Darren said, though Harvey guessed he only wanted to keep him company.

Harvey bent his head over his book.

"I've just thought of something," said Darren, interrupting him.

Harvey tried to read and listen at the same time.

"I think everyone on The Team should get to keep the Floodlights Cup at their house for one week each," said Darren.

Harvey looked up. "Good idea," he said. "But ..." He didn't know how to say it.

"What's wrong with that?" said Darren.

"Nothing," said Harvey. "It's just — I have to study now. I can't talk."

Darren nodded, and Harvey went back to reading his book.

"Wait a minute!" said Darren, grabbing Harvey's shoulder. "Harvey — what was Mr Spot's team called again?"

"They're Finbar Fly's All Stars," said Harvey irritably, not looking up.

There was a silence beside him. Darren was holding his breath.

"What is it?" said Harvey at last.

"All Stars," squeaked Darren. "What does that mean?"

Harvey hadn't thought about it. "It's just a name," he said.

"Or," said Darren, looking terrified, "if Mr Spot used to be a professional, they could be real football stars!"

Harvey was aghast. He hadn't even thought about who would be playing on Mr Spot's team. What if they *were* famous players? It was possible.

"There's no way The Team can win against professionals," said Darren morosely.

Harvey felt a stirring inside him. The Team weren't *that* easy to beat — and they never gave in, not even against sides who were bigger and better than them.

Harvey closed his book as the bell went for the end of lunch. He wasn't thinking about history anymore. He was already imagining The Team facing famous players — and beating them.

"We can win if we're ready," he told Darren that afternoon. Mr Spottiwoode had taken the

class outside again, and was making them catch parachutes he dropped from the roof.

Harvey's mind was humming. If only The Team had an advantage. He looked up at Mr Spottiwoode, and saw him rubbing his back as if he was in pain. Aha! "The All Stars will be old, won't they? They'll be slower than us. We can win if we're sharp, focused and fast."

When the bell rang that afternoon, Harvey shoved his books into his bag and ran home. He studied all evening, and even got up early to study before school the next morning.

"It's going well," he told Darren in class. "I've done History and Geography. I'm doing Maths today, and Science tonight. Here." He handed Darren a note, grinning as Darren read it out loud.

"Midweek Report. You, Darren, are BANNED from talking to Harvey until after the test. Yours sincerely, H. Boots."

Throughout that day, Harvey studied for the test, secretly ignoring Mr Spottiwoode's lessons. He had to join in, though, when everyone left their desks, took off their shoes and dragged them across the floor.

"You've not been missing much," Darren told him. "I don't know why we're doing this. If you ask me, Finbar knows you're going to ace the test, and he's so frightened that he can't teach straight."

During the last lesson of the day, Harvey wrote down everything he'd learned so far — and soon had several pages of facts. He began to feel confident. It didn't matter what size his brain was — if he studied hard, he could learn. All he had left to do was Science, and there was just enough time for it after The Team's training session that evening.

"I've got some great new ideas for The Team, too," he told Darren.

Darren covered Harvey's mouth with his hand. "Sshh!"

Mr Spottiwoode was coming towards them.

"I noticed you working at lunchtime," said Mr Spottiwoode. "You're developing good study behaviour, Harvey."

Harvey met his teacher's gaze. He wasn't scared of Finbar Fly, or his All Stars. He was going to be ready for them.

"He's done History, Geography and Maths already," blurted Darren. "He's going to beat the ban!"

Mr Spottiwoode frowned. "You do know that the test is only on *this week's* topic, I hope?"

Harvey's eyes flicked to the blackboard

behind Mr Spottiwoode's desk, and for the first time all week he read what was written on it. "Forces?" he said.

"Correct!" said Mr Spottiwoode. "And thank goodness for that! For a moment I thought you hadn't been taking any notice of my wonderful lessons!"

Mr Spottiwoode walked away, and Harvey stared after him, numb with shock.

"I thought he said *every* topic," Darren hissed. "I was talking to you about the Floodlights Cup while he was telling the class, and I mustn't have heard properly. Harvey, I'm sorry — I got it all wrong."

Harvey turned to Darren. "What are forces?" he said desperately.

Chapter 5

"I won't be playing," Harvey told The Team that evening as they stood under the brand-new floodlights, which would be turned on for the first time on Saturday night. "I studied all the wrong things and the test is tomorrow, so I'll still be banned. But that doesn't mean The Team can't win," he added.

"Yeah, sure, Harvey," said Matt moodily. "The Team are going to beat a bunch of superstars with our striker sitting on the sidelines. No problem."

Harvey lowered his head. Matt had a point, of course. And not only was Harvey The Team's main goal scorer, without him they'd be a player short.

"What did you forget to study?" said Rita.

"Forces," replied Darren.

"Forces!" snorted Steffi. "They're not so hard. Why don't you just read your notes through a few times? You need to put some effort in and ..."

"I wasn't listening," said Harvey. "I was studying other stuff, so I didn't write anything down."

"Didn't you do any practical experiments?" said Rita helpfully. "Like dropping parachutes, and rubbing your shoes on the ground? Or pulling on a rope?"

"I wasn't watching properly," said Harvey.

"This is the Fly's fault," complained Darren. "It's probably all part of his plan to keep Harvey out of the game. Why didn't he stop us talking?"

Steffi rolled her eyes. "If you're at school, you're supposed to pay attention, not wait for someone to tell you to!"

"Your attitude," said Matt, jabbing a finger at Harvey, "has handed our cup to the All Stars on a plate."

Harvey turned away. Matt and Steffi were right. He should have been listening to Mr Spottiwoode all along. That's what school was for.

"Teacher alert!"

Harvey spun around to see where Matt was pointing.

"It's the Fly!" bellowed Darren. "He's come to spy on us!"

Harvey saw someone sprinting towards them so fast his legs were a blur. All he could make out was a suit and tie — but it wasn't their teacher, not unless his eyes had been replaced with laser lights.

"Better late than never!" called Professor Gertie, hurrying after her robot.

Harvey felt a tingle of excitement run up his back. Professor Gertie had *never* let him down before. She would know exactly what to do.

Mark 1 drew to a standstill in front of Harvey. Behind him, he could hear The Team chuckling. The robot was dressed in a brown corduroy jacket, brown shirt and brown spotted tie. Even his trousers were brown.

But it wasn't only his clothes they were laughing at.

"Why's Mark 1 got a moustache?" said Darren.

Professor Gertie ignored him. "I decided Harvey might need some last-minute help to make sure he gets top marks in his test. So I've invented the ultimate solution to everyone's study worries. Let me present ... Mark 2 — the Teacher Machine!"

"Rrrready to rolllll!" chimed the robot, punching the air with both fists.

The Team fell silent. After a minute Rita said, "It's just Mark 1 with funny clothes, right?"

Professor Gertie pursed her lips. "In a manner of speaking," she admitted, "yes. But he's much improved. I have taught him everything I know."

"Can he teach me about forces?" Harvey said eagerly. "I need to learn them — and fast."

Professor Gertie put her lips to the Listener on the side of Mark 1's head and said loudly, "Harvey Forces Teach Fast!" Then she stood back, grinning. "Just give him a moment to prepare himself. Mark 2's head is no longer a space for fishing line and marbles. It is now bursting with useful new circuits, mega-memory chips, nanobotic doo-dahs, and —"

Without warning, the robot's head fell backwards, and a football popped out.

Professor Gertie — and most of The Team — screamed.

The robot bent down, and Harvey saw inside the rubbish-bin head. It was completely empty — except for the Pea Brain. Then the Football Machine's head flipped back into place with a *click*!

"All my effort wasted!" wailed Professor Gertie. "He's got football on the brain!"

"Hey Mark 1," said Harvey. "You're back."

"Heyyy Harvvv," said Mark 1. He put the ball into Harvey's hand. "Let's playyy!"

Harvey dropped the ball to his feet and kicked it towards Rita. "The Team might as well practise," he said dejectedly. "I'll just watch from the sidelines."

"Okay —" Rita began, but as she stooped to collect the ball, Mark 1 snatched it up. He brought it back to Harvey, and began whining loudly in his ear.

Harvey cringed. Mark 1's voice sounded like a badly tuned radio on full volume. It made his head hurt.

Desperate to get rid of the sound, Harvey threw the ball to Steffi. Immediately, Mark 1 leapt towards her, knocked her out of his way, and grabbed the ball again.

"Hey!" yelled Steffi, rubbing her arm. "Professor! Your robot's lost his marbles!"

"Why's he acting like this?" hollered Harvey as Mark 1 screeched at him.

Professor Gertie hung her head. "I don't know, Harvey," she said miserably. "It looks like the Teacher Machine is a failure, and so am I!" Shaking her head sadly, she walked away.

Harvey saw that Steffi was leaving too.

"What about training?" he called, as he watched The Team drift away. He could hardly hear himself over the sound of Mark 1, who was now whirring like a drill. Harvey's head began to throb.

Suddenly, Rita, who'd been watching Mark 1 curiously, ran over and banged the robot three times on the top of his head. Then she screamed into his Listener, "Harvey Forces Teach SLOW AND QUIET!"

"And sso," said Mark 1 gently, "your kick iss the force thatt makes the ball begin to move. Repeat pleaze."

Harvey gaped.

"You'd better repeat it," said Rita.

"My kick is the force that makes the ball begin to move," said Harvey.

"Quite sso," said Mark 1. "And gravity is the force that pulls it downwards to the ground."

"He's teaching you about forces!" said Rita. "I knew it!"

"And I'm learning!" Harvey replied, beaming with relief.

The next morning, Harvey sat at his desk with the test paper in front of him. His fingers were trembling nervously as they gripped a pencil.

Mark 1 had spent all evening teaching him. He'd followed Harvey home and sat with him through dinner. At bedtime, Mark 1 had left, only to return a short time later dressed in pyjamas and carrying a sleeping bag. He continued to talk into Harvey's ear while they both brushed their teeth, and then crouched by his bed, whispering about forces even as Harvey was falling asleep, exhausted.

When Harvey awoke that morning, he'd discovered the robot lying next to him. Harvey had been using one of his feet as a pillow. The Teacher Machine was still and silent at last, and Harvey supposed he'd already told him everything he knew about forces. But had Harvey really learned it?

"Begin," said Mr Spottiwoode.

Harvey started to read through the questions — and his pencil fell to the floor with a clatter.

He didn't know the answers.

His head felt as empty as Mark 1's.

Chapter 6

Harvey could hear Darren scribbling away next to him.

"If I don't know the answer," Darren had told him before the test started, "I'm going to make something up."

I'd better do the same, thought Harvey as he bent over to pick up his pencil.

Something fell out of his ear. It bounced on the classroom floor and, without thinking, Harvey caught it in his fist. It felt prickly. He opened his hand. It was Mark 1's Pea Brain.

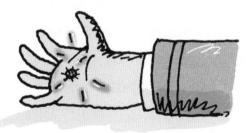

No wonder he hadn't been able to wake the robot up before he came to school — Mark 1 wasn't sleeping at all. He was OFF, because he'd given Harvey his *brain*.

Harvey thought about putting it in his other ear to see if it would work there, but he decided not to. He knew that Mark 1 had meant well, but using an extra brain would be cheating — and that was worse than anything, even failing.

Harvey put the Pea Brain on the desk in front of him. He could still hardly believe that everything Mark 1 knew was contained in such a tiny brain. Apart from knowing about forces — and everything else Professor Gertie had taught him — Mark 1 had taught himself to talk, juggle, and even invent things. And on top of all that, he was a football genius.

Harvey thought of the amazing shot Mark 1 had been trying to teach him for ages. He had to kick underneath the ball, to make it spin. That way, the air resistance made it move slowly and …

Harvey sat up in his seat. Air resistance — that was a force, wasn't it? He found the question at the bottom of the page.

What force slows an object as it moves through the air?

Harvey wrote, "Air resistance."

He read the question above the one he'd just answered.

What force pulls objects to the ground?

Harvey wrote, "Gravity." He felt his heart speed up as he answered one question after another. It was like he was skipping past defenders and heading straight towards goal. He was doing it! Soon there was just one question to go and—

"Time's up!" said Mr Spottiwoode and Harvey looked up. The Fly was standing right next to him, watching him. "Please stop writing," he said. "And well done, class."

Harvey put his pencil down as Mr Spottiwoode picked up first Darren's paper, then his.

Harvey felt light and happy. He was sure he'd done well on the test — and now he'd have the chance to beat the best goalie in town.

Chapter 7

In the last lesson on Friday afternoon, Mr Spottiwoode gave back their corrected test papers. Harvey had passed with his highest-ever mark — nine out of ten — and it felt as good as winning a match. Mr Spottiwoode had written, "Excellent. The ban is lifted. But keep it up — winners work hard."

One–nil to me, Harvey thought.

After school, Harvey returned Mark 1's brain and arranged to meet the robot for a training session the next day.

On Saturday, Harvey got up late and spent the afternoon on the field with Mark 1. He was in top form, and when he scored his tenth goal in a row against the robot, his confidence was fully restored. The Team couldn't lose. The cup was theirs.

"I'm ready," Harvey told himself calmly as he walked towards the field on Saturday night. "Ready for anything."

Turning the corner out of Baker Street, Harvey saw that the floodlights were now glowing white and magical in the night sky. A line of children and their parents were walking towards them. Harvey heard a boy say, "I'm going to see Finbar Fly!" and a girl reply, "So am I!"

When Harvey reached the brightly lit pitch, he guessed there were at least two hundred people already gathered. He saw The Team gaping at the size of the crowd. Steffi looked more furious than he'd ever seen her.

"I can't stand it!" she said. "Everyone seems to know what the Fly is, but they won't tell me. Even my teacher knows!"

"Your *teacher*?" said Harvey.

"There are loads of them here," said Darren suspiciously. "If you ask me, we're being set up."

"What for?" said Harvey.

"Think about it," said Darren. "They've got Finbar Fly here to attract a crowd. He's their hero, and they don't want to see him lose. So who do they choose to play against him?"

"Who?" said Matt, scratching his ear.

"Us!" said Darren. "A bunch of kids! We don't stand a chance," he finished sulkily.

Somebody coughed, and Harvey saw that Mr Spottiwoode, hardly recognisable in a silver goalkeeper's jersey, was standing behind Darren.

Darren spun around and goggled at their teacher's huge gloves, then at his even larger boots. Finbar Fly seemed about ten feet tall. The Team looked terrified.

Harvey spoke up. "We do have a chance," he said quietly. The Team all turned to him. "*If* we work hard," he added.

"And that's why I chose you to play against me," Finbar Fly said to Harvey, his moustache bristling in what Harvey took to be a smile. "I know you can work hard when you want to."

The ref blew his whistle and everyone who wasn't playing left the pitch. Harvey saw Professor Gertie and Mark 1 standing on the sidelines. The professor was looking mournful, and Harvey realised he'd forgotten to tell her how Mark 1 had helped him. She probably still thought her Teacher Machine was a disaster.

Rita grabbed Harvey's arm. "Look what we're up against!" she said fearfully.

"What's wrong?" said Harvey, surveying the All Stars. As he'd hoped, they were all old. "Some of them look like they've never played football before!" he said. He could feel his heart beating strongly as he waited for the whistle.

Three All Stars attackers lined up right in front of them, before the ref explained that they weren't allowed inside the centre circle. Harvey chuckled. The All Stars were a joke!

"See the tall one with long hair?" Rita said. "That's my teacher, Miss Kwong. Next to her is

Matt and Steffi's teacher, Mr Slack. And that," she said, pointing to a gigantic figure standing like a rock in the All Stars' defence, "is Mrs Quake, our school headmistress."

Harvey looked hard at Finbar Fly's team, and recognised some more teachers from his own school. Darren was right — they had been set up! But their teachers were about to find out how good The Team could be.

"Let's keep the ball to ourselves!" he called to his team mates. "We'll control the game!"

Harvey kicked off to Rita and, with a bellow, Miss Kwong launched herself at them. Rita sidestepped her and knocked the ball to Matt, who passed to Steffi, who sent it gliding back to Darren in goal.

"Short passes, no risks!" Harvey encouraged his team mates.

It was almost like a practice session, Harvey thought. The teachers were wearing themselves out as they chased after the ball, and The Team were soon relaxed and enjoying themselves.

"This is fun!" said Steffi, slipping the ball between Mr Slack's legs and collecting it herself. "We're in charge for once!"

"Mine's very well behaved for her age," commented Rita, giggling as she left Miss Kwong standing.

"I'm giving *my* teacher a gold star!" said Matt, narrowly avoiding being tackled by Mr Slack before he toe-poked the ball to Harvey.

Harvey made his first run upfield — and was promptly flattened by Mrs Quake.

"Sorry, dear," she apologised. "But there *is* a silver cup at stake, after all, and I'm quite determined to win it!"

The teachers began to use their size advantage, barging The Team about in midfield. Harvey was starting to feel frustrated — The Team hadn't had a shot yet. He saw Finbar Fly yawning as he leaned lazily against his goalpost. Time for a test, Harvey decided.

Rita made a run, drawing the defence with her, before back-heeling the ball to Harvey, who saw that Mrs Quake was out of position. Without a moment's hesitation, he whipped a shot towards goal. Skimming low across the grass, it was as far from Finbar Fly as could be.

The legendary goalie took two steps, then launched himself towards it. There was a loud gasp from everyone — even Harvey. Mr Spottiwoode looked like he was flying!

His hands closed on the ball, he rolled over twice, then stood up gracefully and bowed.

But that was nothing compared to what happened next.

Mr Spottiwoode drew back one of his gigantic feet and booted the ball high over

Harvey's head. Harvey twisted around and saw it shining like a shooting star as it sped across the sky. It was heading straight for The Team's goal.

Darren, who was off his goal line, ran backwards, trying to shield his eyes from the dazzling floodlights. He jumped, flapped at the ball, got his fingers to it, lost it, then crashed to the ground as it bounced into the net.

Harvey watched open-mouthed as Mr Spottiwoode cartwheeled towards the corner flag. The ref blew his whistle like a steam engine and called, "Half-time in the Finbar Fly game! Finbar Fly scores!"

The crowd was chanting. "The Fly! The Fly! The Finbar Fly!"

Harvey felt empty. So *that* was the Fly. It wasn't a save — it was a shot.

Steffi marched over to him, her face livid. "Why didn't you know about the Fly? I suppose you and our butterfingers goalie were too busy messing about in class when he told everyone!"

"Nobody at our school knew," said Harvey defensively. "We can still get back in the game though. We need to work harder and —"

"YOU need to work harder," said Matt, poking Harvey in the chest.

"What's that supposed to mean?" said Darren, coming up to stand shoulder to shoulder with Harvey.

"He's *your* teacher," argued Steffi.

"So *you* have to save his shots, Darren," declared Matt.

"And," Steffi ordered, "YOU have to score, Harvey Boots!"

Chapter 8

"Do you ever get the feeling that everyone is against us?" said Rita as she sat down with Darren and Harvey in the centre of the pitch. "Even my dad's hugging Finbar Fly now, and he should be on my side!"

"I'm really, really sorry for letting in that goal," said Darren, thumping the ground with a gloved hand. "I just wasn't expecting it. Do you think you can score?" he asked Harvey hopefully.

Harvey shrugged. "We've got to keep trying," he said.

"The problem is," said Rita, "if you shoot and miss, your teacher will be able to try another Fly."

"I'm ready for him," Darren said in a determined voice. "He only scored last time because I couldn't see."

Professor Gertie came over, her hands thrust deep into her lab coat pockets. "I wish I could help," she said dismally, "but I didn't dare invent anything else in case I made things worse. I'm a complete failure. It might be safer if I give up inventing altogether and become a teacher instead. Like your Mr Spotty."

But Mr Spottiwoode wasn't a failure, Harvey thought. He was the greatest goalie ever, and he'd chosen to become a teacher instead because he'd really wanted to be one.

Harvey remembered that he had something to tell the professor. "Your Teacher Machine was excell—" he began to say, but Professor Gertie had wandered away as Mark 1 came striding towards them.

"She's avoiding him," Rita said. "Doesn't she realise Mark 1's her greatest success?"

The robot opened his mouth and spat two things onto the grass in front of them.

"He's giving me the creeps," grumbled Darren as Mark 1 skipped away backwards. His mouth was still wide open as he sang loudly, "Happee Birth-dayyy, doo doo!"

"We'd better open our presents," said Rita, unravelling a wrinkly yellow baseball cap. "Look at this!" she exclaimed. "Something to shade your eyes, Darren!"

Darren snatched the cap and put it on, calling gratefully, "Thanks, Mark 1!"

Harvey unfolded the second of Mark 1's gifts. It was a white T-shirt which had words written on it in black crayon.

"It looks like my little brother wrote on it," said Rita. "Or someone else who hasn't been to school yet."

Harvey read aloud, "Farts baa wartyup?"

Darren snorted. "No, it's *Farce* ba warty you."

Rita giggled. "It says, *Force be with you!*"

"Well that solves everything," said Darren sarcastically, flinging the T-shirt into the crowd on the way back to his goal for the second half.

Harvey looked around for the rest of The Team. He didn't have time to work out Mark 1's message — he needed to fire up his team mates, who looked like they'd already lost the match.

"Make sure we keep the ball," he urged them. "But this time, we attack!"

Matt clapped slowly, saying, "Great speech — not!"

But the rest of The Team looked like they were willing to try.

As the All Stars kicked off, Harvey noticed the Floodlights Cup was now displayed on a table by the centre line, glittering like a diamond in the light.

Then he took the ball from Miss Kwong as she thundered past him, and began The Team's assault on Finbar Fly.

Don't shoot, Harvey told himself as he neared the All Stars' penalty area. He could have sent the ball bending around Mrs Quake, who was looming in front of him, but to beat Finbar Fly he'd need to be closer.

Mrs Quake barged into Harvey and the ref gave Harvey a free kick. It was still too far out, so he chipped the ball towards Steffi, who was running in. She headed low and central, but Finbar Fly saved it easily with his feet.

The Team piled on the pressure. Rita's wicked back-heel would have fooled any other keeper, but not the Fly. Even Matt joined in, trying a spectacular diving header. Unfortunately, his head connected with Finbar Fly's stomach instead of the ball, and the ref gave him a yellow card.

"Five minutes to go!" shouted Rita's dad.

"Harvey!" called Rita. "We need to score — and now!"

Harvey screwed up his face, trying to think. Everything he knew from playing the game, and all Mark 1's training, was useless against the Fly. What else could he try?

He saw Mark 1 hopping up and down on the sideline. He was wearing the white T-shirt, and pointing frantically at its message.

Farts baa wartyup, thought Harvey. *Force be with you.* His foot provided the force that made the ball move. If only he could kick with more force, the ball would go faster …

Suddenly Harvey realised that there might be one way to beat Finbar Fly. It was time to try something new.

Rita had a corner.

"To me!" Harvey called urgently, and The Team gathered around him.

Harvey quickly explained his idea.

"This had better work," said Matt as they took their positions in front of the All Stars' goal. "Or you've lost us our cup."

Rita jogged across to take the corner kick. She took a run up, and The Team suddenly darted towards her, calling for the ball. As Harvey had hoped, the All Stars followed The Team, while he sprinted back to the goal area to face Finbar Fly alone.

Rita whipped the ball in hard towards Harvey, who saw Finbar Fly spread himself in the centre of his goal, his eyes wide as if he knew what Harvey was planning. Harvey had to kick the ball before it bounced. If he did, *the full force of Rita's cross would be added to the force of his own shot.* Harvey drew back his foot and—

BANG!

He was knocked backwards as the ball rocketed towards goal. Blinking, he watched Finbar Fly explode towards the top corner, his long fingers stretched — but they weren't long enough.

Hardly daring to believe that he had beaten the Fly, Harvey started to raise his hands. And then—

THWOCK!

The ball slammed against the crossbar, and Harvey stared in horror as it bounced onto the goal line — and straight into the waiting hands of the Fly.

Finbar Fly stood up, and fired.

Harvey closed his eyes. This time he couldn't look. He'd been so close to scoring, and now — thanks to another famous Finbar Fly — the All Stars were going to score again.

The spectators were silent. Darren let out a long roar. "Nooooo!" Then the ref's whistle screamed for the end of the game. The Team had lost. And Harvey Boots had failed again.

Chapter 9

Somebody skidded into Harvey, knocking him flat on to his face. He turned over and saw Darren standing over him. Harvey had no idea why Darren was beaming. "What a game!"

"We lost," Harvey told him simply.

"I know," said Darren, looking regretfully towards the Floodlights Cup. He turned back to Harvey. "Shame about that, isn't it?"

Harvey thought the Fly must have hit Darren on the head. "Why are you smiling, Darren?" he said gently.

"Because I feel happeeee!" squealed Darren. "I know the Fly beat me the first time," he explained. "That felt like getting a double detention. But I learned my lesson, and the second time, I was ready for him." Darren clapped his hands above his head. "SWAT!"

"You mean you saved the Fly?" said Harvey.

Darren shook Harvey violently. "Yes! And he's not a bad shot, is he, our Mr Spot? I'm actually quite proud to have him as a teacher. When you think about it, he does try to make the lessons interesting. From now on, I'm going to listen to him sometimes. I think you should too, Harvey."

As Darren carried on telling him how he was going to concentrate more at school, Harvey looked around. The Team were chatting happily with the All Stars as if they'd won, not lost. Harvey couldn't understand it.

Rita came running over. "Harvey, you were brilliant!" she said, chortling. "Did you see how we tricked them?"

"Great shot, Harvey!" said Steffi, kicking one of Harvey's boots as she and Matt walked past. "We've got no complaints."

"It was unstoppable, mate," said Matt, holding out a hand to help Harvey to his feet.

"Darren, Rita," Harvey pleaded. "You *didn't* win a silver cup. None of us did. The Team *failed*."

"Yeah," said Rita. "But only just."

"You know what I think?" said Darren, chewing his lip thoughtfully. "I think failing now and then is a good thing."

"How do you work that out?" said Harvey.

"Well," said Darren. "You were failing at school, and it made you work harder. Now you know loads of stuff you didn't know before."

"He's got a point," said Rita. "Losing always makes The Team try harder — and get better."

Professor Gertie marched up, with Mark 1 following close behind. "Super game!" she said. "And you did your best, Harvey, your very best. You know, Rita's right. From now on, I'm going to look at my failures as the stepping stones to my wonderful success!" She linked arms fondly with Mark 1, who tried to wriggle away. "Who cares if my inventions don't always do *exactly* what I want them to? My Marky's perfect, just as he is. I'm so proud of him!" She kissed the robot on the top of his head before he could pull free.

Harvey saw Finbar Fly climb on to the table to show off his trophy.

Mr Spottiwoode had *never* failed, thought Harvey. He'd wanted to be a teacher, and he was a good one, too. He even knew how to stop Harvey from failing — by telling him the truth, and making him work harder.

The crowd gasped as Mr Spottiwoode began wobbling dangerously. Then, with a cry, he toppled, dropping the Floodlights Cup. He dived to retrieve it — but missed. A hand Harvey recognised scooped it up, shoved it inside his shirt, and bounded away.

One person began to clap, then another, until suddenly the whole crowd was applauding.

"That kid dives like an *eagle*!" bellowed Rita's dad.

"He's my boy!" said Professor Gertie adoringly, wiping a tear from her eye.

Harvey flung back his head and whooped triumphantly. "Even the Fly's a failure sometimes — he's not perfect!"

"Too true!" said his teacher, springing to his feet. He looked happier than Harvey had ever seen him. "You very nearly beat me. And Darren is one of the few to save a Fly. Congratulations, both of you!"

Harvey saw that Darren was blushing with pleasure.

"Teacher's pets," commented Steffi good-naturedly.

"How about my All Stars play The Team again next year?" suggested Mr Spottiwoode.

The Team, and their teachers, all cheered.

"More failure!" said Darren, rubbing his hands together gleefully. "I can't wait!"

Harvey shook his head, though. In his mind, he saw his shot again, zooming past the Fly's outstretched fingertips. If he had kicked *under* the ball, the way Mark 1 was teaching him, the air resistance would have helped to drop it under the crossbar, and into the net.

"Losing might be good for us," said Harvey. "But next year — we win!"

MASTERS OF SOCCER

Chapter 1

"*What* did she say?" said Harvey.

It was Monday afternoon assembly, and Harvey had just watched four girls do a dance called *Sleeping Beauty*, which had sent him into a comfortable doze. Now Mrs Pinto, the Headmistress, was talking, but Harvey was yawning so much he couldn't hear her.

"After School Clubs," Darren replied, shaking his head. "It's an experiment — we have to join a club and meet every afternoon this week, starting today."

"School after school?" said Harvey in disbelief. "What about The Team?"

"Looks like soccer training is off," Darren said moodily.

Mrs Pinto, who was small and bean-shaped and had a high, singsong voice, began to read from a list. "The topics available to students are as follows," she said, clearing her throat. "Kitchen Dynamics. Fabric Awareness. Frontier Exploration."

Harvey heard Rekha whisper nearby, "I think she means Cooking, Dressmaking and Science."

Darren pulled an ugly face to show what he thought of them.

"And last but not least," sang Mrs Pinto, "Sporting Development."

"Huh?" said Darren, looking hopeful but unsure.

"Sports," said Rekha, and Darren shouted "Yes!"

Mrs Pinto peered around the hall before continuing. "On their way out, each student must sign up for their preferred A.S.C."

"After School Club," translated Rekha.

"If a club becomes full," said Mrs Pinto, "please sign up for your second choice. Then proceed to the assigned meeting place. Clubs will begin immediately."

Harvey and Darren scrambled to their feet at the same time. There was no point in hanging about, Harvey knew. They needed to get their names down, and fast.

Darren was the first to line up in front of their teacher, Mr Spottiwoode, who had "Sporting Development" written on a sign hanging around his neck.

"We're doing sport," said Darren and Harvey together, grinning.

Mrs Pinto spoke from behind them. "I'll take these two, Mr S."

Harvey and Darren spun around.

"Follow," said Mrs Pinto, and she headed off at a brisk pace.

Harvey and Darren looked at each other. Harvey shrugged. "We must have done something wrong," he said. "She's not taking an After School Club, is she?"

"Come along, lads!" came Mrs Pinto's call. "Never be late for an important date!"

"I've got a bad feeling about this," whispered Harvey as they waited outside Mrs Pinto's office. Their headmistress had disappeared inside without a word, and it sounded like she was moving chairs and tables about.

Just then, Harvey saw the girls who'd performed *Sleeping Beauty* dance along the long corridor towards them, talking excitedly.

"What now?" said Darren suspiciously, but before anyone could answer, Mrs Pinto opened her door wide.

"In you go!" she chimed, and the girls tiptoed after her.

Harvey and Darren stood side by side in the doorway, peering in. The dancing girls had lined up along one wall, standing with their arms in the air and one leg sticking out. Mrs Pinto was sitting at her desk, which was pushed tight against the wall, leaving a large space in the centre of the room.

"Step up!" said their headmistress, and Harvey and Darren drifted in reluctantly.

Without thinking, Harvey let go of the door, and it swung shut behind him with a worrying *snip*!

"Welcome," Mrs Pinto declared, "to Ballet Extravaganza!"

Darren made a strangled noise. "Nyeear!"

"Pardon?" said Mrs Pinto.

"I think he means ..." began Harvey, but he couldn't go on. His legs felt weak, and he began to sway. He felt Darren's hand clasp his. It wasn't holding hands, thought Harvey. They were just holding each other up.

"Well, never mind," said Mrs Pinto. "As I was saying, this is Ballet Extravaganza, or B.E., as we shall call it."

Harvey's hand was being crushed. He could feel Darren trembling.

"I bet not a single person in this school knows that before I trained to be a teacher, I was —" she smiled, "a ballerina!"

The girls erupted into shrieks. "Oh, Mrs Pinto!" said one of them.

Harvey and Darren began to edge backwards. Please, door, don't be locked, Harvey thought.

"I have waited for years to use my ballet skills to train a troupe of my own."

Harvey's elbow touched the door. Darren was nearest to the handle. They began to turn around slowly, careful not to draw attention to themselves.

"What I needed was a 'corps de ballet', a group of dancers — and that, ladies, is you."

Harvey heard the girls whimper with pleasure. Darren silently turned the door handle.

"I have also invited a Dance Master to choreograph a special dance for us," said Mrs Pinto. "That special person will be arriving tomorrow."

Darren gave the door handle a mighty tug. Nothing happened.

Harvey put his lips to Darren's ear and said shakily, "Yank the handle *up* to unlock. You have to —"

"And, most important of all," came Mrs Pinto's voice, "I had to find two strong, capable boys."

There was an ominous silence. Harvey and Darren twisted around to face their headmistress.

"Please, Mrs Pinto," begged Harvey. "We don't know anything about ballet."

"Which is perfect!" cried Mrs Pinto. "You are the empty page upon which our dance shall be written!"

"But we can't dance," pleaded Harvey.

"We've got blisters!" said Darren wildly.

"No need to worry," Mrs Pinto soothed. "Today we're just doing the dressing-up bit. That's mostly for the ladies — you two only get to wear these boring old things."

What she handed to them was red and stretchy, and looked to Harvey like a swimsuit.

"Er, you've given us the girls' ones," he pointed out.

Mrs Pinto took the outfits back, and held them up. "No, no," she said. "They have your names on them."

It was true. Harvey saw that each swimsuit had a name tag sewn on to it. They were for Harvey Boots and Darren Riley.

"Leotards aren't easy to get on first try," said Mrs Pinto. "So take your time. You may change in here."

She opened the door to her storeroom, handed Harvey and Darren their leotards, and waited patiently as they shuffled inside.

Mrs Pinto switched on the light, and closed the door.

Darren was shaking all over with fear.

Harvey felt his legs buckle, and he collapsed to the floor.

"You've got five more minutes, lads!" called Mrs Pinto. "Then we'll all see how lovely you look!"

Chapter 2

"Got to … get out," Darren said. It sounded like his jaw was frozen.

Harvey looked high and low. There were no windows, just a small grille high up near the ceiling, but it was far too small for anything bigger than a cat to squeeze through.

Darren began clawing towards it with both hands, his legs trying to climb the smoothly painted wall.

"It's no good," Harvey said. "There's no way out."

Darren's head whipped around; he spotted a cupboard, and threw himself at it, wrenching open the doors.

"One minute more!" called Mrs Pinto.

The cupboard was filled with books, which Darren scooped out frantically.

"Ten more seconds!"

"There's no point hiding," said Harvey, trying to calm Darren down. He'd never seen anyone panic like this.

Darren pressed himself into the cupboard space just as Harvey grabbed the doorknob, which had begun to rotate. He couldn't stop it moving.

"Five, four, three, two — *ta-da!*" Mrs Pinto pulled open the door so forcefully Harvey was propelled into the office outside. The girls tittered.

Mrs Pinto pursed her lips as she looked first at Harvey, and then at Darren squashed in the cupboard.

"Oh, silly lads!" she said, tutting. "I suppose you might as well keep your school uniforms on for our first few lessons, until you overcome your shyness."

A hot feeling of relief rose from Harvey's toes to his head, making him feel as light as a feather.

Darren emerged, red-faced, but Harvey could tell he was back in control.

Mrs Pinto raised her leg into a kick. The girls copied her. Harvey and Darren watched.

"We're waiting, lads," said Mrs Pinto.

Harvey lifted one leg. Darren lifted his foot.

"Now like this," said their headmistress, raising her arms above her head to make an oval shape.

The girls did the same. So did Harvey, wobbling on one leg. Darren put his hands up as if he was tipping a shot over the crossbar.

"Good, good," said Mrs Pinto, who seemed pleased with them, and Harvey felt his spirits lift. What they were doing wasn't the nightmare he thought it would be — not yet, anyway.

Mrs Pinto checked her watch. "Our time is up, alas. But we shall meet again tomorrow."

Darren grabbed Harvey by the elbow as he marched past. "Out of here," Harvey heard him mumble.

"Just one more thing!" said Mrs Pinto as they reached the door. "B.E. is a *secret* club. Anyone who spills the beans will be answerable to ME."

She unlocked the door for them, and stood aside to let them out.

"As if we'd *tell* anyone!" Darren said angrily, under his breath.

They had trudged halfway along the corridor before Mrs Pinto called, "Repeat the exercises before bed each evening. Hard work really does pay off, you know. And you will need all the practice you can get for the performance."

Harvey and Darren stopped so suddenly they might have run into an invisible brick wall.

"A performance!" said one of the girls.

"Do you mean it?" said another excitedly.

Mrs Pinto was beaming with pleasure. "Yes, my dears, it is quite true. We will be performing in front of the whole school on Friday morning!"

With a muffled cry, Darren sprinted away. Harvey, faint with terror, did the same, and didn't stop running until he'd reached the safety of Baker Street.

There was no way he and Darren would dance in front of the whole school. Never.

But right now he couldn't think of any way for them to get out of it.

Chapter 3

Harvey's house was at the top of Baker Street. Next door, there was a tower shaped like a rocket about to take off. Professor Gertie, who was an inventor, lived there with her greatest invention, the football-playing robot Mark 1.

The best thing about having an inventor living next door, Harvey decided when he woke up on Tuesday morning, was that inventors knew how to fix problems. Fixing problems was what they did best.

Before leaving for school, Harvey knocked loudly on the tower door. There was a furious clattering coming from inside. It sounded to Harvey like an elephant typing on a keyboard.

There was no answer.

Harvey banged louder. The clattering stopped.

"Hey!" called Harvey. "I know you're in there!"

There was a long silence.

"Professor!" called Harvey. "I —"

Professor Gertie's face appeared at an open window, and Harvey hurriedly told her about Ballet Extravaganza. "And then on Friday we have to perform in front of everyone," he finished. "Though of course, we won't."

"Why not?" said Professor Gertie curtly.

Harvey goggled at her, amazed. Perhaps she didn't understand. "It's … *ballet*!" he said. "And we're *boys*."

"Boys do ballet," said Professor Gertie. "I don't know what all the fuss is about."

"But —!" said Harvey.

Professor Gertie frowned and blinked. "The thing is," she began, beckoning Harvey closer as if she was about to tell him a secret. "I'm not supposed to, but …" Suddenly, Professor Gertie shook herself, and her voice became sharper. "No, I can't. You'll just have to go with the flow, Harvey. All I can say is, hard work really does pay off. Got that?"

Harvey opened his mouth, but couldn't speak. Those were exactly the words Mrs Pinto had used!

"Later, alligator," said Professor Gertie, with a wave goodbye as she slammed the window shut.

"Later," breathed Harvey, totally confused. Professor Gertie was behaving strangely — very strangely. And as Harvey headed off to school, he was beginning to wonder why.

When Harvey arrived in the classroom Darren was sitting at his desk looking like he didn't have a care in the world.

"We're sorted," Darren said, giving Harvey the thumbs up.

"You mean we don't have to go back to …" Harvey lowered his voice as he sat next to Darren, "B.E.?"

"Oh, we'll be prancing about all right," said Darren lightly. "There's no way Pinto will let us out of it — not if she can help it."

"Then how are we sorted?" said Harvey.

"We take Friday off." Darren leaned back and rubbed his hands together, satisfied.

Harvey thought about it. It sounded like a good idea — if they could get away with it, that was.

"How can we?" he asked curiously.

"No problem," said Darren. "I only have to tell my mum I've got a sniffle and she makes me go back to bed. I had the most days off in the whole school last year, remember."

Harvey nodded, recalling how proud Darren had been when he'd found out.

"What about me?" Harvey said.

"You stay over at my place," said Darren. "The next morning, we both say we're going to puke, and we both go back to bed. My mum will be even more worried about you. There's no way she'll send you to school."

Harvey smiled. It sounded easy — too easy, almost.

"The only bad part is that we have to hop about in Pinto's room for three more afternoons. But at least we're only doing it in front of the Sleeping Beauties, and they're not allowed to tell anyone. That's the main thing, Harvey. *Nobody will know what we're doing.*"

The classroom was filling up, and Darren lowered his voice.

"We should try to look like we're enjoying it," he said. "That way, Pinto won't suspect anything, and it will be a big surprise for her when we're not there at the very *silly* B.E. performance."

"B.E.?" Paul Pepper was standing over them. "What's that?" he demanded. "And why weren't you two at Sporting Development?"

He raised his voice so that everyone could hear. "Sounds to me like Harvey and Darren are doing Fabric Awareness! Or is 'B.E.' even more of a joke?" Paul Pepper cackled, and to Harvey's dismay he saw Rekha look at them over her shoulder, mouthing "B.E." to herself and frowning.

Harvey's heart began to race. He was sure Rekha was about to guess what "B.E." meant, but in the end she just gave him an odd look before turning away.

Darren was definitely right. The main thing was that nobody would ever know what they were doing. If they did, he and Darren would never live it down.

Chapter 4

Darren strode along beside Mrs Pinto, with Harvey and the Sleeping Beauties behind. There was nobody about — the other After School Clubs were being held in a different building.

"I hope we haven't got too far to go," Darren said airily. "Because I don't want us to waste time when we could be, you know, wagging our knees about and stuff like that."

Mrs Pinto took a sharp left into a classroom. Darren hesitated. It was pitch-black inside.

Click!

Light flooded the almost-empty room. Harvey, joining Darren, saw right away why it had been so dark. Large lengths of brown paper had been taped over the windows.

"It won't be a surprise performance if everyone already knows what we've been up to," said Mrs Pinto with a wink.

"Perfect for keeping our secret," Harvey said to Darren.

Harvey began to relax when Mrs Pinto asked them to line up for the first exercise without even once mentioning leotards.

And then he heard heavy, clumping boots coming along the hallway.

"Hide!" said Darren, his good humour gone. "We can't be seen here!"

They crouched behind a pile of chairs.

The footsteps grew louder, then, right outside the room, they stopped. There was a *whirr*, a creak, and a low hum as Mark 1, the Football Machine, entered the room.

"Everyone, please welcome our Dance Master!" chimed Mrs Pinto.

"Hi-ho," the robot said in his strange, mechanical voice.

"Is Mark 1 going to teach us ballet?" said Harvey incredulously as he and Darren emerged from their hiding place.

"Yes indeed!" said Mrs Pinto. "He comes highly recommended."

"By who?" Harvey asked bluntly, sure that he'd already guessed the answer.

"Oh, you know," said Mrs Pinto lightly. "He was revealed to me by a rather *inventive* new friend of mine."

Harvey had a sinking feeling. There was no doubt about it. Professor Gertie was involved. And knowing her, she'd planned everything from the start. But why? She and Mark 1 were always one hundred percent behind Harvey. What could possibly have turned them against him?

Harvey shook his head to clear it. That couldn't be right. Professor Gertie had never let him down. There had to be some other explanation — though Harvey couldn't imagine a good one.

Suddenly, Mark 1 bent so far over backwards he could place his hands on the floor. Harvey thought he looked like an upside-down, four-legged spider.

"Ouch," said Darren. "That looks painful."

"Nonsense," countered the headmistress. "You'll be doing that yourself by the end of the week. Now, there's just one more thing we need."

With a flourish, she picked up a large plastic shopping bag that Mark 1 had brought in, and tipped out the very last thing Harvey expected to see.

It was yellow and fluffy, but there was no mistaking what it was.

"Why have you got a football, Mrs Pinto?" he asked, picking it up.

Mrs Pinto took it from him. "Let's find out, shall we?" She made as if to walk away, then turned suddenly and said, "Heads, Harvey!" Swinging her arm wide, she launched the ball straight at him.

Caught by surprise, Harvey just managed to nudge the ball with his head, directing it back to his headmistress.

"It's really soft!" Harvey said, amazed. It had felt like heading a sponge.

"It's a Squishy Squash — a ball specially invented for indoor use," said Mrs Pinto.

Professor Gertie again, thought Harvey. "Squishy Squash" was just the kind of name she would give to one of her inventions.

"We will use the Squishy Squash so that we don't smash windows or hurt anyone. Darren — catch!" Her arm extended again, this time sending the ball high over their heads.

Darren leapt for it, but the ball slipped through his fingers.

Harvey couldn't help snorting. "Sorry," he said. "But it was a bit butterfingers, wasn't it?"

Darren looked hurt, but their headmistress was beaming. "That's the idea!" she said. "You almost had it. You just need a little more *poise*. A touch of *finesse*."

"A touch of what?" said Darren, perplexed.

"Throw to me," ordered Mrs Pinto.

Darren scooped up the ball and tossed it to her casually. Harvey was sure he had aimed it deliberately wide. Then, to his astonishment, the headmistress plucked the ball from the air with an enormous leap, landing lightly on her toes with the Squishy Squash held between her tiny outstretched hands.

Someone was clapping. Harvey looked towards the girls, but it wasn't them. Nor was it Mark 1, who was sitting cross-legged on the floor, thoughtfully pressing his button.

Darren clapped again, hands above his head. "Awesome save, Mrs Pinto," he said, his eyes wide.

"I don't get it," said Harvey, shaking his head. "Are we doing ballet, or playing football?"

"You will be exploring ball-based skills through the medium of balletic dance," said Mrs Pinto. "Let's begin."

When Harvey headed home that evening he was thoroughly confused. They had been doing B.E., which he was supposed to hate, and yet he felt as if he'd just been in the best football training session ever. Darren had made some incredible leaps to catch the Squishy

Squash, sometimes even managing to land gracefully on one foot. It was perfect practice for The Team's goalkeeper.

Harvey had found he could knock the ball whichever way he wanted it to go with any part of his foot, even the sole, if he used his arms to balance.

Meanwhile, Mark 1 had demonstrated tackle moves to the Sleeping Beauties, who were quick learners, and probably good enough already to try out for The Team.

Harvey's whole body was aching, but that was good. It meant his muscles were working hard. And hard work really did pay off.

Harvey stopped, thinking of Professor Gertie again. He was outside her tower, but all was silent. Cupping his hands around his mouth, he called, "What's going on, Professor?!"

He waited for an answer, but instead he heard a piercing shriek from up the street.

Turning, he saw Rita, his attacking partner on The Team, pedalling her bike towards him, waving and spluttering words so fast he couldn't understand a thing.

She fell off her bike and began limping towards Harvey, holding one of her trainers, which had slipped off.

She was almost breathless with excitement. "COMING!" she gasped. "HERE! PEDRO MANOLO IS COMING HERE!"

Rita sat down on the kerb, took a huge, steadying breath, and told Harvey again what she'd already told him twice.

"Pedro Manolo is coming to your school on Friday."

Harvey's mouth was hanging open. His eyes had glazed over, and he hadn't blinked for some time. Pedro Manolo was the greatest sportsman on the planet. Everyone knew that.

"He's just been named World Soccer Star for the fifth time in a row," said Rita, "and now he's on tour. Are you all right, Harv?"

"Yeah," said Harvey, whose whole body had gone numb.

"There's some kind of show on in the morning," Rita went on. "I don't know what it is, but all my school is coming to see it. Pedro Manolo will be there. Then there's lunch, and after that, a Manolo Soccer Masterclass!"

Rita stood up. "I have to go," she said. "I just wanted to tell you as soon as I found out, because Pedro's your hero, isn't he?"

"Oh yeah," said Harvey.

"Are you really okay?" said Rita, concerned. "You don't look well. Try to get a good night's sleep. You don't want to miss school on Friday."

"I'll be there," said Harvey, trying to sound cheerful.

As he watched Rita cycling away, he realised he had a simple choice. Either he did a ballet dance in a leotard in front of everyone he knew, or he missed the greatest opportunity of his life.

Chapter 5

When Harvey explained about Pedro Manolo's visit, Darren screwed up his face so tightly he looked like a prune that had stayed in the bath too long. He kept on looking like that for at least five long minutes.

"Darren," Harvey urged gently. It was like talking to someone who was sleepwalking — you had to be careful not to wake them up. "Are you all right? The bell's just gone."

They were standing by the school gates, and everyone else had gone into class.

Darren's nose began to twitch. Suddenly, his eyes flew open, and his wrinkles disappeared.

"Any ideas?" said Harvey hopefully.

"I think so," said Darren.

"And …?" prompted Harvey.

"We modify the plan," said Darren, patting his sore cheeks. "First we're sick, and we have to stay home from school. Then, just before lunchtime, we're well again, and we get to see Pedro."

Harvey thought it through. "We miss the performance, but turn up for the masterclass?" He whistled. "You're really good at this stuff," he said, slapping Darren on the back.

Darren shrugged modestly.

A movement caught Harvey's eye. It was Mr Spottiwoode, waving at them from the window. "If it wasn't for After School Clubs, I'd put you in detention!" he threatened.

"Oh no!" Harvey joked to Darren. "We wouldn't want to miss B.E.!"

Throughout the day, Darren outlined the details of his plan to Harvey. "We have to be sure we look ghastly," he explained. "And the best way to do that will be to use all the tricks of the trade."

"Rub flour in our cheeks?" said Harvey.

"Of course," said Darren. "And chew some toothpaste so that we're frothing at the mouth."

"Right," said Harvey. "What about hot water bottles — should I bring my own?"

"I've got one you can use," said Darren. And then he balled his fists and said triumphantly, "Pedro Manolo, here we come!"

Wednesday afternoon's Ballet Extravaganza was more fun than any school lesson Harvey had ever had.

He and Darren had both got over the embarrassment of doing jumps and stretches and twirls in front of the Sleeping Beauties, and they put all their effort into following Mark 1's instructions, while Mrs Pinto accompanied their movements on a piano.

It was going to be a match. Harvey and Darren were on different teams, and Darren

kept saving all of Harvey's shots. Harvey flicked the ball all over the place in slow motion, while Darren leapt about catching it. After a while, Darren missed a shot, and Harvey celebrated his goal by twirling around and around and flinging his arms in the air a lot. Then the Sleeping Beauties came on and chased him, spinning a lot too, until they caught him. Eventually, Harvey broke free, raced to the ball, and launched it at Darren, hitting him in the stomach.

After that Darren and Harvey had to do some running and jumping about before collapsing in a heap, chuckling.

"Excellent!" declared Mrs Pinto, as the robot picked them up. "Cut out the giggly bit and we're there!"

The next day, Thursday, they planned to practise the dance twice more — but that afternoon, things started to go badly wrong.

First, at lunchtime, Harvey spotted Professor Gertie talking with Mrs Pinto in the school kitchen.

"Now we know for sure," he told Darren. "Professor Gertie's involved. I can't believe she's let us down like this."

"But she always does the best for us," said Darren, puzzled.

"Not this time," said Harvey grimly.

Darren shook his head. "Stop worrying, Harvey, or you really will make yourself sick!"

Later, Harvey overheard Rekha pondering the meaning of "B.E." with Paul Pepper. "You know," said Rekha, "I'm sure it's something to do with Mrs Pinto's secret class, the one Harvey Boots is doing. You don't think the 'B' could stand for 'Ballet', do you?"

Harvey arrived at their last After School Club feeling nervous and jumpy, as if he was being watched.

"Calm down!" said Darren. "We have to look casual — you'll make Mrs Pinto suspicious!"

Harvey tried to act normal, but all he could think about was how often the simplest plans could go wrong — especially when Professor Gertie was involved. He couldn't concentrate at all, and he yelped, startled, every time Mrs Pinto shouted at him for making a mistake.

"Mr Boots," she said as the lesson drew to a close, "you must conquer your nerves! And don't worry, it will be all right tomorrow, I'm sure."

Harvey and Darren were leaving when Harvey saw it.

There was a tiny tear in the paper that was blocking out the windows, and through the tear he saw an eye.

Darting across, he peered out just as Rekha and Paul Pepper skidded around the corner.

So that was that. Even without doing the performance, everyone would soon know that Harvey and Darren did ballet.

"It could be worse," said Darren morosely, when Harvey told him on the way to his house. "At least we're not going to prance about in front of them tomorrow. I can't even imagine how embarrassing that would be."

But as Harvey drifted off to sleep that night, he had the terrible feeling that they were about to find out.

Chapter 6

The first part of Darren's plan worked like a dream.

With flour-white cheeks, frothy lips and foreheads heated with hot water bottles, they had staggered into the kitchen while Darren's mum was making breakfast.

"We're not well, Mum," said Darren.

"Oh, you poor dears," said his mum, holding a hand to each of their heads to check their temperatures. "You're both burning up! And you're as white as a pair of sheets."

"Day off," Darren mumbled, letting toothpastey froth dribble down his chin.

"Of course," said Darren's mum, and Harvey felt a flutter of relief in his chest.

"Then again," said Darren's mum, "what would Harvey's parents think if I just left him alone and didn't take proper care of him?"

"W-what are you on about, Mum?" said Darren, his voice wavering. "Why can't we just stay at home with you?"

"Because I'll be at your school all day, helping Professor Gertie. She's responsible for the Big Bash Picnic at lunchtime, didn't you know? And we're all going to sneak in to watch the secret performance Mrs Pinto has been preparing."

"We'll be okay here on our own," insisted Darren urgently, and Harvey could see his face creasing up as he tried to change the plan. "I'll look after Harvey, and he'll look after me."

"No, no, no," said Darren's mum. "That won't do at all! I'm not letting either of you out of my sight. You can both come with me to school."

Harvey's guts did somersaults as he and Darren put on their school uniforms, with Mrs Riley calling for them to hurry.

"What do we do now?" he kept saying. "Darren, she's your mum — think of something!"

Darren was grinding his teeth. "I need more time to work things out. Whatever happens, Harvey, we're not doing the performance, so there's no need to worry ..." But he looked more worried than Harvey had seen him in his life.

"Come on, boys, you're late!" called Darren's mum.

"We're being sick, Mum!" called Darren desperately.

"Oh, tosh!" she replied.

Darren looked horrified. "I don't understand it," he said to Harvey. "She doesn't believe me!"

"Tosh," repeated Harvey heavily. "That's another thing Professor Gertie says. She's behind all this — and I think we're about to find out what she's been up to."

When they finally went downstairs, Darren's mum threw them their coats, then led them outside.

It was a beautiful, sunlit Friday morning. Birds were singing in every tree and there was a cool, refreshing breeze. Harvey realised he would normally have been looking forward to The Team's match tomorrow, but this week he hadn't even given it a single thought.

Darren walked with his hood pulled right

down and Harvey couldn't see his face at all. Mrs Riley had to drag him through the school gates.

With dismay, Harvey saw Mrs Pinto waiting for them in the shadow of the hall where her After School Club would be performing.

We have to persuade her that we're ill, he thought desperately. It's our only chance.

He half closed his eyes and tried to look feverish, when all of a sudden Darren threw back his hood and declared happily, "Mum! We're not poorly anymore — we're cured!"

"No!" yelled Harvey, digging Darren in the ribs, but it was too late.

"The fresh air did it!" said Darren, who still hadn't noticed Mrs Pinto. "We're as fit as fiddles! So you can leave us right here and go do your Big Lunch thing and we'll be okay."

Darren leaned over to Harvey and whispered, "We'll have to keep our heads down, and —"

"My boys!" said Mrs Pinto.

Darren's face turned to wax as Mrs Pinto took them each by the arm and led them into the empty hall. Harvey began to shudder as they arrived backstage.

"We're really very, very shy," Darren said to her tearfully, but Mrs Pinto only ruffled his hair.

"I know, dear," she said. "But the show must go on!"

The crowd came in, and the music began.

The Sleeping Beauties were standing on the far side of the stage, peeping through the curtain and squealing with delight.

Harvey and Darren were on the near side, huddled together and trying to keep out of sight. How Mrs Pinto had got them to change into their leotards, Harvey couldn't remember, but he thought it was probably because they had run out of excuses.

Neither of them could think of anything to say, so they stood in silence.

The Sleeping Beauties lined up, the way they had practised. The piano grew louder, and with a crash of cymbals the curtains were drawn back. The girls began their opening dance.

Harvey heard some laughing, and then what appeared to be a bored silence.

The music changed. Their time was coming.

A door beside them opened. The first thing Harvey noticed was that sunlight was streaming in. It was a way out.

Then he saw Professor Gertie enter, hot and flustered.

"Almost — total — disaster!" she said, panting. "Didn't know you were at Darren's. Looked everywhere. Need to give you — these!"

She threw Harvey and Darren their red Team shirts, white shorts and socks. "Hope you didn't think we'd embarrass you with those *leopards*."

"I think she means leotards," Harvey whispered to Darren as they frantically pulled on their football kit.

It was like his second skin, Harvey thought, and he immediately felt more confident, and braver, as if he had the whole Team beside him.

"Good luck!" said Professor Gertie, standing with her arms folded and beaming at them.

Harvey heard the music change again, getting ready for the part where he and Darren would begin.

Harvey's legs seemed to know the routine and, without thinking, he took a step forward.

"No," Darren hissed, holding him. "Let's run!"

"Okay," said Harvey, but he didn't move.

"Now!" said Darren, grabbing Harvey's elbow.

Harvey stayed where he was. His whole body had been trained, ready to move when the music said it had to.

Darren was goggling at him. "You can't do it," he said, his lower lip quivering. "Harvey — it's *ballet*!"

Harvey's heart was racing. "I know," he said. "It's just — we're good at it, Darren."

It felt like he was talking about The Team playing football, because it was the same thing. They had worked so hard …

"Everyone knows we did Ballet Extravaganza," he told Darren. "This is our chance to show them that it's not as daft as they think."

Darren turned away, and strode to the door just as the music played their cue.

"Now!" Harvey said, as he had when they'd been practising.

He heard Darren's fast footsteps.

"I'm on my own," Harvey thought, his whole body erupting with goose pimples as he leapt gracefully onto the stage in front of his hero Pedro Manolo, and just about every person he knew.

Chapter 7

The bellow of laughter was like a sudden blast of wind. Harvey lost his balance and knocked into Darren's shoulder, which thankfully put him back on course to catch the Squishy Squash that was already flying through the air towards him.

Darren? Harvey's head snapped around.

Darren was there beside him, looking like he was in complete agony as he twirled, arms flicking wide, to the far side of the stage.

The audience seemed to draw in a huge breath, and then the bellow came again. "HA! Ha ha ha ha ha ha ha ha!"

Harvey, who'd dropped the Squishy Squash to his feet, mis-kicked, and the ball flew far to one side of Darren. But with a tremendous leap, The Team's keeper collected the ball in his two outstretched hands, landed effortlessly on one foot, and sent the ball arcing perfectly back to Harvey.

The spectators fell silent.

Harvey shot at Darren again, better this time, and he heard an "Ahh!" from the crowd as Darren jumped straight up to let it fall into his outstretched palm.

To Harvey's astonishment, there was soon applause each time Darren saved, and when the time came for Harvey to score, there was a rumble of "Boo!" from half of the spectators, and a cheer of "Yes!" from the rest.

Harvey twirled about the stage, celebrating his goal. Each time he outmanoeuvred the

Sleeping Beauties who were chasing him, he heard a "Whoa!".

There was a cry of anguish when Harvey finally booted the ball into Darren's stomach, and excited calls as he and Darren did their prancing about before falling to the floor to the sound of thunderous cheers.

Harvey and Darren were in a fit of giggles as the music stopped.

"It was okay!" Harvey said.

"It was incredible!" said Darren.

"*Magnificent*!" came Mrs Pinto's voice.

Harvey saw Pedro Manolo walking towards them, and he and Darren stood up.

"He'll never believe we're really football players," Harvey said sadly. "That's the worst bit of all."

Pedro Manolo held out his hand — and then he did the last thing Harvey could have imagined. He started to twirl, spinning faster and faster until he was a blur. Then he stopped, grinned, and shook Harvey and Darren by the hand, before taking two gold medals from his pocket.

"These two students," he said loudly, "have shown themselves to be both brave and skilful — they are Masters of Soccer!"

He hung a medal around each of their necks as the crowd went wild.

Harvey felt like he was dreaming.

"Gold," said Darren, awestruck, nudging him in the ribs. "Not bronze. Not silver. *Gold*."

Harvey, who was staring open-mouthed at his hero, saw Professor Gertie skipping up to them. "Oh, Pedro!" she said, giving the greatest-ever sportsman a kiss on the cheek. "Didn't I tell you they could do it?"

"You did, señorita," said Pedro with a nod, as he was led away by Mrs Pinto, who wanted his autograph.

"You knew about everything!" Harvey accused Professor Gertie, his voice furious and happy at the same time. "I bet it was all your idea, wasn't it?"

"Oh, well, you know," said Professor Gertie mildly. "I just couldn't help myself, not after I read Pedro's book. Have you seen it? It's all about how he secretly used ballet training to help him be as good as he is."

"You're kidding," breathed Darren. "Pedro Manolo pranced about?"

"Ever since he was your age," said Professor Gertie, folding her arms with satisfaction.

"But if you'd told us that in the first place ..." Darren rolled his eyes in frustration.

"I wanted it to be a wonderful surprise for you," said Professor Gertie innocently.

"It was," said Harvey with a sigh.

The hall was emptying, but The Team were holding back to talk to Darren and Harvey.

"Absolutely," began Matt.

"Totally," added Steffi.

"Brilliant!" finished Rita.

"But hurry up," said Matt. "I think I can smell our Big Bash grub burning."

"That'll be my mum's cooking," admitted Darren.

"Yikes!" Professor Gertie bounded away. "My kebabs!"

The Team sat with Pedro Manolo through lunch, as he explained the message in his new book, *Soccer Extravaganza*.

"My friends," he told them, "there is just one thing I need to tell you. Hard work —"

"Really does pay off," chorused Harvey and Darren. "We know."

"You've read the book already?" said Pedro.

"We know somebody who has," said Harvey, smiling.

Just then Paul Pepper came up with his own team, the Diamonds. "Is everyone going to be shown football ballet now?" he asked, making sure he was first in line.

"My two experienced teachers will show you everything they know," Pedro promised.

"Where are they?" said Paul Pepper, looking around.

Pedro put his hands on Harvey and Darren's shoulders. "Here."

Paul Pepper blinked. "Come on, then," he said, grumpily. "What are you waiting for?"

Harvey saw that Darren was glowing with pride — and knew he was too.

Just then, Mark 1 arrived, carrying a jumble of what looked like girls' swimsuits.

"I spent days clacking away at my old sewing machine," said Professor Gertie busily. "But I should have enough leopards for everyone."

With great pleasure, Harvey held out the first leotard for Paul Pepper.

"We'll start with the dressing-up bit," he said, and it wasn't long before he and Darren had to hold each other up again — only this time it was because they were laughing so much.